David Higham Associates
FILE COPY
Publication Date: _2nd April 2007_

Fat Chance

REASONS FOR ADORING GABRIEL:

1) His face!!
2) His eyes!!
3) His lips (when smiling or otherwise)!!
4) His hair!!
5) His smooth, suntanned, muscly six-pack. . .
6) . . .in fact, his smooth, suntanned, muscly bod in general!!
7) His *cough* bum!!
8) His sense of humour!!
9) His name!!
10) He can drive. And gives his sister lifts, so is kind.
11) He likes animals, so is kind and sensitive.
12) He speaks French. Fluently. So is clever, kind and sensitive :o)
13) He skis. And snowboards. So is sporty, clever, kind and sensitive :o) :o)
14) Oh stuff it. Just HIM!!! HE ROCKS!!!!!

Look out for Catherine Robinson's other titles:

Tin Grin
Celia
Mr Perfect
Soul Sisters

www.catherinerobinsonbooks.com

Catherine Robinson

Fat
Chance

■SCHOLASTIC

*For Caz, Stacey, Lette, Polly, Charlie, Vicki
and all the MKP-ers – girls, you rock!*

First published in the UK in 2007 by Scholastic Children's Books
An imprint of Scholastic Ltd
Euston House, 24 Eversholt Street
London, NW1 1DB, UK
Registered office: Westfield Road, Southam, Warwickshire, CV47 0RA
SCHOLASTIC and associated logos are trademarks and or registered
trademarks of Scholastic Inc.

10 digit ISBN 0 439 94384 1
13 digit ISBN 978 0439 94384 0

British Library Cataloguing-in-Publication Data
A CIP catalogue record for this book is available from the British Library
All rights reserved

Typeset by M Rules
Printed by CPI Bookmarque Ltd, Croydon, Surrey
Papers used by Scholastic Children's Books are made from wood grown in
sustainable forests.

1 3 5 7 9 10 8 6 4 2

www.scholastic.co.uk/zone

Chapter One

The thing with the long school holidays, I find, is that they're almost always a disappointment. You look forward to them practically from the moment term begins, and then after a few days of enjoying not having to get up or go to bed at the normal times, no homework, no nagging teachers etc. etc., you start to get this strange sense that something's missing. That things aren't quite in the groove you're used to. General aimlessness and creeping boredom begin to set in. In short, you start – and I can hardly believe I'm admitting this – *missing school*. Weird, but true.

Take the latest summer holidays, for example; the ones just after GCSEs. It was a couple of weeks in, hot as hell, and I was sitting moodily at the kitchen table with nothing to do and only Molly to do it with. Moll's generally OK company as little sisters go, which was just as well seeing as we were stuck with each other: all my mates live miles away and were anyway doubtless busy with other stuff, and Jaz, Best Mate Extraordinaire and the person I really wanted to be spending time with, was on holiday in France with her folks. Which accounted for the moodiness – mine, at any rate. Moll was doing her best to be positive and think of things to occupy us, but frankly her up-beatness was beginning to grate.

"Let's go down to the cove and have a swim," she enthused. "It's so nice and warm today, it'll be great."

"No it won't. It'll be full of tourists."

"Exactly." She gave a little giggle and tossed her hair. "You never know what talent we might spot."

I stared at her. When did my baby sister turn into a sex kitten? Besides, what right-thinking almost-sixth-former goes on the pull with a thirteen year old?

"I'm not in the mood."

"Oh." She sounded disappointed but didn't try to persuade me, just nibbled on her thumb, thinking. "I'll henna your hair for you if you like, I think there's some left in the packet from when I did Chloë's the other week."

I wrinkled my nose. "Bleurgh! You've got to be joking. That stuff stinks worse than Geoffrey's compost heap."

"OK then, I could French-manicure your nails for you. Or you could do mine," she added, without much hope.

"Oh wow. Thrills a-go-go."

"There's always Monopoly. Or. . ." She went over to

the ancient wooden cupboard next to the Aga, bent down, and began to rummage around in it. "Cards?" Her face peeped over the cupboard door, beaming brightly, as she waved the pack in the air like a fan.

I just looked at her, and sighed meaningfully.

"Well, OK then, *you* suggest something." She chucked the cards back, stood up and folded her arms across her chest. "I don't hear you coming up with any brilliant suggestions of things to do."

"I don't want to *do* anything. Why should I have to *do* something? Why can't I just sit here and—"

"Be a miserable old bag?" she interrupted, pulling a face. "Why are you being so grumpy?"

"Because bloody Jaz has gone to bloody France." I sighed again and hoisted my feet up on to the chair opposite, listlessly. "For four bloody weeks. And we have to stay here in Brandy bloody Bay."

"Well, don't take it out on me. It's not my fault your mate's parents can afford to take her off on swanky holidays, and ours can't."

At which point the kitchen door opened and in came Mum, wearing one of her shapeless kaftans and a slightly irked expression.

"Girls, girls! Why are you bickering on such a beautiful day?" I hate it when she accuses us of bickering. It's such a silly word. Arguing is fine; even fighting is OK. But bickering makes us sound so *petty*.

3

She glided over to the window, the kaftan making her appear to be on castors, and peered out of the window. "Look – look at that sky! Not a cloud! It's the sort of day that makes you feel glad to be alive!"

"Yeah, yeah," I muttered. Any minute now and she'd burst into song. "Whatever." I poked crabbily at the marmalade jar with my forefinger, pushing it as far across the table as I could reach without actually changing my position.

"Her bezzy mate's on holiday and she can't function without her," Molly informed Mum brightly.

"Oh, just put a sock in it, will you," I growled out of the side of my mouth, shoving the salt and pepper pots over to join the marmalade. The salt hit the side of a rush mat and tipped over, depositing its contents grainily amongst the coils of the mat.

"Mattie! Now look what you've done!" Mum sprang over to the table and, picking up a pinch of the salt, threw it over her left shoulder.

I looked at her in bafflement. "What are you doing that for?"

"It's seven years' bad luck if you don't. Or is that breaking a mirror? I can never remember." She picked up the mat and carried it to the sink. "Is that why you're in such a bad mood – because Jaz is away?"

"I'm not in a bad mood. I'm bored. Bored, bored, *bored*."

"Yes, you are, you're in a shocking mood. And only boring people say they're bored," she added, trying to sound crisp and disapproving but failing. She doesn't really do crisp; she's so used to being ultra-reasonable about everything that she just ends up sounding depressed.

She tipped the salt in the sink and gave the mat a little bash with the heel of her hand, as if wishing it were me she was knocking some sense into. I knew how she felt. If I was her I'd have wanted to knock some sense into me, too. Trouble was, I couldn't seem to shake myself out of my mood. The heat wasn't helping, either.

"That's Mattie," Molly chirped up. "Boring, boring, boring!"

I glared at her. "I don't know why you're so full of the joys."

"Don't wind your sister up, Molly," Mum chided her, replacing the mat and the salt pot on the table. She turned back to me. "If you really can't find anything to do, you can come to Sainsbury's with me when Geoffrey gets back with the car. I could use a hand."

Monopoly, cards and now *Sainsbury's*! Would the suggestions of thrilling things to do never end?

"Must I? Where is Geoffy Baby, anyway?" I looked around the kitchen as if expecting my stepfather to materialize from inside a cupboard or behind the bin.

"He's taken Rupert to the orthodontist in Exeter. The appointment was for nine – I can't think what's keeping them this long." She cast an eye to the clock above the door, and then back to me, still sitting at the breakfast table in my pyjamas. The implication was clear: *gone twelve and not dressed yet. . .*

"All right, all right," I complained, standing up. "You don't have to say it. I'll go and have a shower."

"I wasn't going to say anything of the kind. But there is something else you could do once you're dressed, seeing as the idea of helping with the shopping is obviously not a winner."

"What?" I said, without much enthusiasm. My mother's ideas of Fab Things To Do In The Holidays include stuff like face-painting or making muffins – OK when you're about eight, but she's never seemed to grasp the fact that both Moll and I had grown out of all that kind of thing centuries ago.

"According to Mrs Potter in the post office, there's a new vicar at Combe Bridge." Mrs Potter-in-the-post-office knows all the goss for miles around. Though why Mum thought this bit of info would be of any interest to me, I couldn't imagine.

I yawned. "Well, if Mrs Potter said it then it must be true."

Across the table from me, Molly sniggered.

"Mrs Potter says he's got a daughter your age," Mum

went on, ignoring my sarcasm. "She'll be going in to the sixth form at St Mark's in September, the same as you. I thought you might pop over and say hello to her. It would be a friendly thing to do, don't you think? Well, think about it, Mattie, at least – don't just stand there with that annoying look on your face!"

She had finally managed to summon up a smidgen of exasperation, and I rolled my eyes. "OK, OK. I can't help my face, can I?"

"Yes, you can. You could try smiling, rather than scowling." She patted my cheek. "Come on, darling. I understand you're missing Jaz, but you can't just sit around being grouchy and doing nothing until she's back. You've got to find something to occupy your time."

I didn't see why. I'd been quite happy just sitting at the table. It was everybody else who seemed to want me to do something. I didn't want to get into an argument with Mum about it – it was too hot, and arguing was altogether just too much effort – but it was clear that lounging around for the rest of the day wasn't going to be an option. It was either Sainsbury's, or the new vicar.

I caught Molly's eye. "What d'you reckon?" I said. "You fancy going over to Combe Bridge with me after lunch?"

Molly shrugged. "I don't mind. It's got to be better

than staying here with you in this mood, hasn't it? I've had more fun watching paint dry."

Combe Bridge is about nine kilometres away and where Jaz and Moll and me go to school (along with about eight hundred other kids, natch) – but apart from the school, and the church that gives the school its name, there's naff all there. This doesn't seem to stop the tourists flocking there in the summer, however, despite the fact that the beach is stony and virtually non-existent at high tide, and all the gift shops sell exactly the same variety of made-in-Taiwan tat. Today was a case in point. The pavements in Fore Street were heaving with holidaymakers: fat women in skimpy T-shirts and unflatteringly tight shorts, middle-aged men in vests, jazzy Bermudas and sandals with socks, and all wearing floppy sunhats against the unusually fierce midday heat. I don't know what it is about being on holiday that makes the British dress so appallingly.

"Why do people bother coming here? Our beach at Brandy Bay is much better," Molly observed as we got off the bus.

"Ssh! Keep your voice down!" I hissed. "We don't want any of this lot turning up on our patch."

"Why not?" She looked around, genuinely baffled. She has no mean side, my sister – it's one of the more annoying things about her because it makes it almost impossible to wind her up. She always sees the other person's point of view; it's something she's inherited from Mum. "What's wrong with them?"

"What's *wrong* with them?" Did I really have to spell it out? "Well, just look at them – their clothes!"

Molly looked. "So?"

"*So?* They're minging." I searched for a way to explain as we walked the few hundred metres along the main street to the church. "Put it this way – how would you feel if Mum went about dressed like that, or Geoffrey?"

"Geoffrey does," she said.

"Well, yeah," I conceded. "Fair point." Our step-father has always been sartorially challenged. Mum does her best with him, bless her, but when her back is turned he still slips back into loafers with no socks, or hideously patterned tank-tops. Having no fashion sense is deeply embedded in his genes, as it is with his son Rupert, who actually turned up to meet us all for the first time (I'm talking ages ago now, of course) in school uniform. Yeah. Exactly.

"Don't be such a snob, Mat," Molly said. "People can wear what they want, specially when they're on holiday."

"Yeah, I know they can. Of course they can. I'm only saying – *Jesus*!" I exclaimed, stopping dead. "Look at that!"

"What?" Molly looked around exaggeratedly. "What have you seen now? Some woman who's daring to wear a top you disapprove of? A man whose socks are too last season?" Her clear voice carried across the still summer air, and I grabbed her by the arm and pulled her behind one of those people-carrier things that was parked on the road just opposite the vicarage's drive.

"Something much more interesting than that. Look – across the road. In the garden. *There*, Molly, for Christ's sake! Look!"

She looked. She saw. She stood open-mouthed – just as I had done – because what she spotted was just about the hottest boy I'd ever seen in my life. He was a couple of years older than me, judging by the look of him, and dressed in a pair of frayed, stonewashed cut-off jeans and nothing else. His arms, legs and smooth muscled torso (oh my God, that six-pack. . .) were tanned the colour of butterscotch; his hair was either bleached by the sun or else naturally pale golden-blond, like wheat standing in the fields, worn dead straight and slightly too long, like a French footballer's, and pulled back into an elastic band at the nape of his neck. He was pushing a lawnmower – the old-fashioned, non-electric kind – across the front lawn of the vicarage in a desultory fashion with one hand and holding a book with the other, and the sight of him made my mouth water. I swear to God – I actually salivated, standing there watching him.

He was clearly having much the same effect on Molly. "Oh man," she breathed, in awe. "Major hottie alert!"

"Hands off – I saw him first," I told her. Suddenly, the day seemed much brighter. I peered round the back of the people-carrier and stepped off the kerb.

"Where are you going?" she squeaked anxiously.

"Where d'you think? To say hi, of course."

"You can't!"

"Whaddya mean, I can't? Why can't I?"

"You can't go and chat up the vicar's gardener!"

"Why not? Just give me one good reason."

"Because – because you can't!"

"That's not a reason, it's a tautology," I informed her snootily.

"Call it what you like. I know you when you're in this mood, you get *way* embarrassing. Anyway, what if the vicar comes out while you're doing your 'I'm So Sexy' thing?"

"What if he does? I'm only planning to say hello to the guy, not rip my kit off and rugby-tackle him down on the grass with me. Although come to think of it. . ." It was quite a pleasant thought, but Molly was scandalized.

"Mattie! What are you like? Don't you dare go over there!"

Don't you dare? Who did she think she was, Mum? I ran my fingers through my hair, licked my lips and stepped determinedly into the road. "Watch and learn, Sis," I instructed her over my shoulder. "Watch and learn."

I sauntered across the road, half willing and half dreading him looking up and noticing me. Despite my front with Molly, hitting on lads really isn't my style. I'd like it to be; I'd really love to be one of those super-cool, super-confident girls who say what they like to whom they like. A girl, in fact, like Jaz, who always has her pick of the guys (and in case you're wondering, she's also really pretty, really brainy and really nice. In fact, if she wasn't my best mate, I'd probably hate her). But sadly, I'm not like that. Put me in close proximity to a hottie and you can usually rely on me to have an acute attack of foot-in-mouth disease. Either that, or I turn into a mumbling, blushing fool. Which is probably what Molly meant when she said I was embarrassing.

I had to show her, though, didn't I? It was my duty as her big sister to give her a masterclass in chat-up technique, even if I was normally lousy at it. But today felt different. I felt recklessly devil-may-care; I had nothing to lose, and besides, Molly was still on the other side of the road. She wasn't actually going to hear what passed between us.

By the time I got to the garden gate, Mr Buff the Gardener had come to a standstill with the lawnmower and was deep in his book. I wondered how much the vicar was paying him to cut the grass. Whatever it was, he was being ripped off. On the other hand, Mr Buff did make a bloody good garden ornament.

I coughed, he glanced up, and I nearly fell over. His eyes were the deep velvety-brown of the centre of pansies, and fringed with long, luxuriant eyelashes like tropical bird-eating spiders. It was almost indecent for a man to have eyelashes that thick; it would have taken about five applications of mascara to make mine look like that.

I swallowed, my bottle suddenly deserting me. "Hi," I croaked.

He smiled (*Oh my GOD. . .!*), and marked his place in the book with a forefinger. "Hello."

"Erm. . ." I croaked again, and cleared my throat. "I was just wondering. . ." It came out as a husky squeak.

"Are you OK?" He lowered the book and craned his neck to look at me, and the movement made his six-pack flex. I closed my eyes to block out this vision of loveliness. How could I concentrate on making the right impression when he rippled his bare muscles in front of me?

"Yeah," I mumbled, and shuffled my feet. This wasn't quite turning out as I'd intended. I gave myself a little

13

inner shake. *Come on! Get a grip!* I coughed. "Yeah, I'm fine." Normal voice. That was better. "I was just wondering whether you happened to know if the vicar was around? Or – or. . ." I struggled to stop burbling. "Or in, at all?" I tried to smile, but it came out all lop-sided, and the smell of cut grass started to tickle my nostrils, making me want to sneeze. *Great! First burbling, now facial contortions – I must be coming across as a total freak.* But if I was, he didn't appear to notice. He smiled back, a soft, gentle smile that spread slowly across his face. God, he was truly, heart-stoppingly gorgeous.

"I'm not sure," he said. We stood there for a moment, he with his finger still marking his place in the book, me just drinking in his awesome beauty. Well, that and trying not to sneeze.

"Oh," I managed, at last. "Shall I go and ring the doorbell, then?"

"That would probably be best." He smiled again, closed his book and laid it on the grass. Then he loped lazily across the lawn, leaving the mower where it stood, while I admired his rather fetching back view.

"So he didn't ask you for a date then." It was a statement, not a question. Molly had materialized beside me.

"Not quite yet."

"Did you get his name?"

"Er – no," I confessed. Then I caught sight of his

14

book, still lying beside the lawnmower. "But I tell you what – he's not just a pretty face. That's Proust he was reading. In French!" I was well impressed, but Molly just wrinkled her forehead.

"What's Proust?"

"It's not a what, it's a who."

Molly's forehead wrinkled even more, giving her the look of a puzzled chimp. "You've lost me. Give me a clue."

"It's – oh, never mind. Just take it from me, he's got brains as well as beauty."

Just at that moment somebody came round from the side of the vicarage where Mr Buff had disappeared. Somebody dressed in crumpled linen trousers and a dad-ish cardigan, in spite of the sweltering heat; somebody with the small white band of a dog collar visible at the neck of his pale blue shirt. I felt suddenly guilty, as if I'd been caught doing something naughty. I instinctively stood up straight, and dug Moll in the ribs with my elbow.

"Eh up," I hissed. "It's the vicar."

"Hello ladies," he greeted us as he came across the lawn. Close up, he had a slightly anxious, distracted air about him. "Were you looking for me?"

"Er, yeah. Kind of."

He came up to the gate and offered us his hand over it. "I'm Peter Foxcroft. The new vicar of St Mark's," he added, a bit unnecessarily, given that he was standing on the inside of the vicarage gate.

"Yeah, we realized that – the dog collar kind of gave it away." I meant it as a joke, a merry quip, kind of thing, but his worried look increased, as if he thought Molly and I might leap over the gate and accost him. Luckily, my manners clicked in at that point and saved the day.

"I'm sorry," I said formally, shaking his hand. "We're Matilda and Molly Fry. We go to St Mark's – the school, I mean – and I'm going to be in the sixth form next year, same as your daughter."

"So we thought we'd pop by to say hi to her," said Moll. "Well, not pop exactly. We came on the bus, it's about half an hour away. We live in Brandy Bay," she added.

"Do you? And you've come especially to see Rebecca? How incredibly kind of you." He sounded genuinely chuffed; he smiled, and looked suddenly much younger. It's something I've noticed before with, erm, more mature people. (Memo to self: remember to smile a lot when you get old.) He also reminded me of somebody, but I couldn't think who it was.

I gave a modest smile. "Oh, that's OK. So is she in? Er, Rebecca?"

"Ah." He looked apologetic. "I'm afraid she isn't. She's – um – popped out. Shopping. Or something."

He waved a vague hand. "You've had a wasted journey. Terribly sorry. But maybe you'd like to come in anyway? Have a cup of tea, or. . .?"

He left the sentence hanging in the air, and Molly and I exchanged glances. Tea with the vicar hadn't really been on the agenda, even though to refuse meant passing over the possibility of catching another glimpse of his tasty garden staff.

I pulled what I hoped was a regretful face. "We ought to get back, really. Our mother will probably be wondering where we've got to." Beside me, I heard Molly draw breath in preparation to contradict me. I gave her another, more discreet, dig in the ribs. "Perhaps you could tell Rebecca we came round?"

"Of course," he said, and smiled again. "She'll be in tomorrow, I believe, if you feel like coming over again? Or perhaps you'd care to telephone? Now – what is that number – I'm afraid I haven't managed to memorize it yet." He patted his trouser pockets uncertainly.

"Oh no, don't worry," I assured him. "We'll call round again, won't we, Moll? Tomorrow morning – say about eleven?"

"Tomorrow. About eleven." He nodded gravely. "Very good. I'll be sure to tell her. And it's Molly and – ?" He looked at me questioningly.

"Matilda. Mattie."

"Mattie. Very good." He smiled once more and turned as if to go, then stopped, his eye caught by the book lying on the grass. "Ah. *À la Recherche du Temps Perdu*," he murmured, and bent down to pick it up, clasping it fondly to himself like a favourite stuffed toy. "I wonder how that got there?" We pulled innocently clueless faces, neither of us wanting to tell him that his gardener had been rifling through his bookshelves. We didn't want to get him into trouble. "How strange. Ah well. Must get on. 'Time's winged chariot', and all that."

He drifted off back round the side of the house, still clutching the book, and Molly and I looked at each other.

I grinned. "Just imagine," I said. "That could have been *Playboy* left lying down there."

"Yeah." She sighed wistfully. "Wasn't he totally gorge, though? Those pecs."

"Nah – not my type at all. I'm not into vicars. Still, whatever floats your boat."

She gave me a playful shove. "No, you dope. Not him – Lawnmower Man. Tell you what, though. That vicar really reminded me of Geoffrey."

Chapter Two

It wasn't Geoffrey he reminded me of. Geoffrey is tall
and lanky and dark and skinny – think daddy-long-
legs, but without the bleurgh factor. When Mum first
met him, at the university where they both work, he
had a kind of dusty, unhealthy sallowness about him,
as if he'd spent far too much time locked up in gloomy
libraries with only ancient academic tomes for
company. Come to think of it, he probably had. Don't
get me wrong – he's OK, is Geoffrey, in a bumbling,
not-quite-of-this-world way. But he's kind, and he
clearly adores Mum, which is the main thing, after all.
(His son Rupert, on the other hand, is more of an
acquired taste. I'll get on to him in a bit.)

But the vicar – Peter Foxcroft – was fair, and kind of
chunky beneath his vicar's kit, and when he smiled
you could tell that he'd probably been quite good-
looking in his day . . . whenever that would have
been. Probably about thirty years ago, judging by his
appearance now.

Mum, of course, wanted to know all the details when Molly and I got back home. Not many families move in to this area: there's retired couples a-go-go, but new families are decidedly thin on the ground. (No work, you see, or none to speak of unless you're a) a farmer, or b) don't mind only working during the famous Tourist Season, i.e. between Easter and when the schools go back in September.) So any new families tend to attract a good deal of interest, of the *Hello!* magazine type – what do the parents do, how old are the kids, what's the house like, etc. etc. Most of which Mum already knew, and what she didn't know we couldn't help her with, based solely on our brief visit.

"We only saw the vicar," I pointed out. "He didn't whisk Mrs Vicar out of his pocket and introduce us."

"And we didn't see Rebecca because she wasn't in," Molly added. "Although her dad did invite us in for a cuppa."

"You should have accepted. I've never been in the vicarage. I'd love to know what it's like inside . . . it looks so beautiful from the road." Sighing dreamily, Mum threw open the pantry door and regarded the contents quizzically.

Moll and I exchanged glances. "Mum," I said, "get a grip. As if we were going to have tea with him! If you were that keen to get the low-down you should have come along too. Tell you what – why don't you come with us tomorrow?"

"Not 'us'," Molly said, shaking her head. "I'm going round Chloë's tomorrow. Looks like it'll just be you and Mum, Mat."

But Mum knew when her leg was being pulled.

"Don't tease," she said. "I'm just saying it's a beautiful house, that's all. Now then. . ." She shuffled a few things around on the shelves and tapped her chin with a forefinger, thoughtfully. "Do you girls know whether the last of the porridge oats have been finished? Somebody seems to have moved the shopping list."

"Where did you leave it?"

"Well, I think it was on top of the microwave. Or it might have been on the front of the fridge. Or possibly stuck to the corkboard."

That was the trouble with our house now – too many people in it for comfort. You couldn't rely on finding stuff in the same place where you left it. On the other hand, Mum has always been terminally disorganized. I strode over to the corkboard and found the list half-hidden underneath a letter from the school PTA dated two terms previously.

"Is this it, by any chance?"

"Oh, thank you, love. That's saved me such a lot of time. Now I just need to round Geoffrey up, and we can get off to Sainsbury's."

"Haven't you been yet? I thought you were all set to go before Moll and me went off to Combe Bridge. That was hours ago."

"He's only just brought Rupert back from Exeter. Apparently the orthodontist's secretary made some kind of mix-up with the appointment times."

At this point the kitchen door opened, and in they both came. Gomez and Pugsley Addams. Actually, I'm being unfair; Pugsley is fat (at least, he is in the movies), and Rupert is skinny as a rake, thin as a pole, scrawny as—

No, no, no. I mustn't go down that road again. Been there, done that, indulged in all the name-calling and the taunts and the baiting, and much good it did me. Rupert and I – well, let's just say we didn't exactly hit it off when we first met. Under normal circumstances we would probably have crossed the street to avoid contact with each other, but as it was we found ourselves shoved into having to share a home, and all because my mother and his father decided they were going to get married.

But all that's in the past. We're never going to be the best of mates – we're far too different; I mean, he's super-brainy for a start – but we just about manage to be civil to each other now. Most of the time. I find it's best all round.

"Hello, girls," Geoffrey said, rubbing his hands

together jovially. He does that a lot. "Alice tells me you've been off making a new friend. Did you have fun?"

"Er . . . not exactly. She wasn't in. I'm going back tomorrow."

"That's kind of you," Rupert said, unexpectedly.

I glanced at him, sensing sarcasm. "What?"

"It's kind of you to go and tell her about St Mark's. Being new's howwid." He turned to look at me. He didn't look as if he was being sarcastic. He even gave me a smile, or what passes for a smile with him: a kind of reptilian upward turn of the mouth. Feeling generous, I gave him the benefit of the doubt.

"Yeah, that's what I thought. Anyway, it's no big deal."

It was only when I was on the bus the following day, on my return journey to Combe Bridge, that I started wondering what on earth I was thinking of. Doing the eighteen-kilometre round trip once to see the new vicar's unknown daughter was fine, but doing it twice because she was out the first time seemed a tad, well, over-keen. I hoped she wasn't going to think I was some kind of Billy No-Mates, with nothing better to do in the summer holidays than go calling on total strangers not once, but twice in twenty-four hours. Or worse, what if she thought I was snooping, coming round to check out the new arrivals?

As I got off the bus I consoled myself with the thought that at least I might bump into the fit gardener again, but there was no sign of either him or any gardening equipment when I opened the front gate and walked up the path. Suddenly feeling as shy as if I were arriving at a party where I didn't know any of the other guests, I rang the doorbell. *Don't be so pathetic,* I told myself firmly. *You're just being friendly. How could anyone possibly mind that?*

But it seemed as though my first instincts had been correct, because the door was snatched open almost before I removed my finger from the bell, and the girl who stood in the doorway had the biggest scowl I'd ever seen since Molly was about four. This girl was tiny – short and slight, dressed in a black spaghetti-strapped top with a blood-splashed skull and crossbones across the front, bleached ripped jeans, and a studded black leather belt hung about with lengths of chain and slung low around her hips. Her upper right arm was encircled by a tattoo of vicious-looking barbed wire. Her heavily mascara'd brown eyes were ringed with kohl, and she had a punky blonde crop whose gelled spikes were tipped with vivid magenta. A fingerless lime-green lace glove – just the one – completed the ensemble. I stared at her, speechless. We don't see many midget rock chicks in our neck of the woods.

"Yes?" she demanded icily.

"Um – is Rebecca in?"

"I'm Rebecca." She scowled again. Small she may have been, but boy, was she scary.

I felt my jaw thud to the floor. She only looked about twelve. If that. I'm not especially tall, but she must have been the best part of a foot shorter than me. "Oh. Right."

"And you are?"

"I'm Mattie. Mattie Fry. I came round yesterday when you were out. Didn't your dad tell you?" Looking down at her, I felt as big and clumsy as an elephant.

There was a moment's silence, then her left hand flew up to her mouth. "Oh bollocks. Yeah, he did. I forgot." She grinned, and the scariness disappeared in an instant. She looked like a cheeky little boy trying to look hard. "Sorry, Mattie. Shall we start again?" She leant against the door jamb and waggled the fingers of her green-gloved hand. "Hi. I'm Bex. *Not* Rebecca, please. It sucks big balls. I mean, tell me honestly – do I look like a Rebecca?"

"Um. . ."

But she clearly wasn't actually expecting an answer. "Look, d'you want to come in for a coffee?" She strode off down the hall, not expecting an answer to that one either. Despite her lack of height, she couldn't half shift. I scuttled after her. "Dad said you're at St Mark's, right? It's dead kind of you to come and give me the low-down. Most people who've been round so far just want to take a look. You know, like we're exotic animals at the zoo or something."

She led the way into the kitchen, picked the kettle up from the worktop and filled it under the tap. A good deal of water splashed out from the spout, over the worktop and even up on to the window ledge behind the sink, but she didn't seem to notice. She plugged the kettle in and opened a cupboard to get mugs out, rattling them around noisily until finding two that met with her approval. "So tell me about it, then. St Mark's. Is it a total shit-hole?"

I blinked. This whole thing – Bex, her look, her full-on attitude – wasn't at all what I'd been expecting. I wasn't sure exactly what I had been expecting, just that this wasn't it. She was a vicar's daughter. How come she was allowed to dress like Courtney Love, and use swear words?

Bex turned away from the kettle. "Well, is it? My last school was – getting away from the place was the best thing about moving. The *only* good thing about moving," she added, and looked at me. "What? What's the matter? Oh Christ, don't tell me – you're shocked. Just because my dad wears a dog collar you think I should dress in nice little cotton frocks and pearls, and say crikey! and gosh!"

Somewhere at the back of my mind a little voice was telling me that shocked was precisely what she'd intended me to be. I pursed my lips thoughtfully, and shook my head.

"Nah. I'm not shocked. It's a free country. Far as I'm concerned, you can wear and say what you like." I smiled at her. "Tell you what, though, I bet you've given all the old biddies of Combe Bridge something to talk about."

She flashed me another grin. "You're not kidding. You want to know something?"

"What?"

"That's why I wasn't here when you called round yesterday. Some old dear from the Mothers' Union had brought a cake round, and Dad was trying to manoeuvre me out of the kitchen and upstairs so that she wouldn't see me. Like the sight of me was going to make her pass out with horror, or something."

It seemed a bit harsh. She wasn't *that* hard-core. Not hiding-away-upstairs-out-of-sight, likely-to-deprave hard-core. I pulled a sympathetic face.

"No way! What did you do?"

"I told him to sod off. Only I didn't say sod. Which probably didn't help, because by this stage Mrs Cake was already in here to see what all the drama was about. Talk about goggle-eyed – she nearly dropped her tin."

"Aw, I bet she loved it. I bet she was off telling all her cronies as soon as she was out the front door."

"Yeah, I bet she was too." Bex sighed. "But Dad threw a total mental once she'd gone. Accused me of being 'Unnecessarily Aggressive' and 'Deliberately Confrontational'." She sighed again. "So then we ended up having a screaming match, until I couldn't stand it any more and ended up storming out."

It was hard to imagine the vicar I'd met over the garden gate doing anything as energetic as screaming. "Yeah? He told me you'd gone out shopping."

"*Shopping*? Yeah, right. Like there's anywhere *to* shop round here." She plonked a mug of coffee down in front of me, along with an open bag of granulated sugar with a teaspoon buried deep inside. "Excuse the heirloom Georgian silver sugar-server, won't you. The sugar-bowl got smashed."

"What, in your row with your dad?"

"No, he dropped it when he was passing it to one of the Mrs Cakes he invites in all the time. They just keep on turning up, all bearing their Madeiras and Battenburgs and what-have-you, and he feels he has to ask them to stop for tea." She took a gloomy sip of her coffee and then looked at me, suddenly apologetic. "Oops. Hope I didn't offend you by saying there's nowhere to shop round here."

"Why should you have? You're right – there isn't."

"Even so. It's still where you live, isn't it? I didn't mean to diss it."

"It's OK. It's not like I've lived here that long myself." I'm not sure why I told her what I did next. Unless it was because she was being so open with me – extraordinarily so, given that we'd never clapped eyes on each other until ten minutes ago – that I felt I should trade confidences in return. "We only moved here about six years ago. My dad used to beat my mum up."

To her credit, she didn't bat an eyelid. "What a bastard. Best off out of it, then. Where did you live before?"

"Manchester. How about you?"

"Windsor."

"Oh, right. Where the castle is, yeah?" I spooned sugar into my coffee and took a sip. "So what made you move?"

Her eyes met mine and a shadow of unease passed across her face, so brief that I wondered if I'd just imagined it. Then she looked away. "Oh, you know," she said, with a shrug. "Clergy families. We get moved round all the time." She indicated my mug of coffee with her head. "You fancy some cake with that? Guaranteed homemade. Just not in this home."

Molly had got wind from her friend Chloë of some kind of scandal surrounding the Foxcrofts.

29

"Chloë's cousin Ash says they had to move away from where they were living before," she told me later that evening, when we were up in the bedroom we share.

"That's because clergy families are always getting moved around."

"No, it's not," Molly insisted. "There's more to it than that. Ash's mum's sister-in-law's got a friend who knows somebody who used to go to their old church."

"Oh well," I said, "not at all second-hand information, then. More like fifth-hand. Hey Moll, you ever heard of that game called Chinese Whispers?"

"I'm only saying there was something a bit suss about the way they left," she said, with a haughty sniff. "Don't believe me if you don't want to."

Why is it that gossip is always so tempting to believe? It seemed too much of a coincidence that somebody from round here should have a connection with their old church in Windsor. But then I remembered the look of discomfort that had passed fleetingly across Bex's face when I asked her why they'd moved, and I did wonder.

"I'm not saying I don't believe you. Just that when there's so many people involved, the truth tends to get a bit . . . well, bent."

She pulled a grudgingly accepting face. "Maybe. I just don't see why people would say things like that if they weren't true."

Boy, did she have a lot to learn about human nature. "Well, if it's true I daresay it'll all come out into the open at some point, won't it? Anyway, if you're that interested, you can ask her yourself. She's coming round for a coffee on Friday afternoon."

Molly pulled a face. "Yeah, right. I'm really going to do that, aren't I? 'Welcome to our little town, Bex, and is it true your dad got kicked out of his last church?' Oh, by the way. . ." She got up from the bed where she was sitting, went over to the desk and picked up a piece of paper. "I nearly forgot. Lisa rang while you were out."

I frowned. "Who? I don't know any Lisa."

"Well, she must know you, or why would she ring you?"

"Search me." I shrugged. "Wait a sec, though. I think she might be that girl Jaz was paired up with last term to do geography coursework." In a school the size of ours there are loads of students you just never get to know, even if they're in the same year as you. But Jaz and I had been in different sets for geography, and I did vaguely remember her mentioning being lumbered with someone she barely knew to do the coursework. "I think her name was Lisa. It might have been Lucy, though, come to think of it."

"She definitely said Lisa."

"No, I meant the girl Jaz did her coursework with might have been . . . oh, never mind." Why is that conversations with my sister can be such hard work at times? "Why was she ringing?"

"Something about a book."

"What?" I couldn't imagine why somebody I didn't even know should be ringing me about a book. "What book?"

"I don't know, do I? It's you she wanted to speak to. Why don't you just ring her back?" Molly handed me the piece of paper. "She left her number. Here you go."

The person I really wanted to ring was Jaz. Not just to confirm that the mysterious Lisa was her coursework partner last term, but just because she was Jaz, my best mate, and I was missing her. We didn't see each other every day in the holidays – she lived too far away for that – but we usually spoke on the phone at least once a day. If she wasn't on holiday I'd already have called her to give her the low-down on Bex and the Rev Dad and Mr Buff the Gardener and a whole pile of other things, and not for the first time I found myself fervently wishing she was back.

I sighed. It was no use wishing: she was still in France.

So I rang Lisa instead, as requested. Rather weirdly, she greeted me down the phone as if we were old mates, even though we'd never spoken before. I still wasn't certain who she was. Her voice wasn't familiar at all.

"Mattie, hi! Thanks ever so much for ringing back. I was just wondering if you could help me out."

"I dunno. What's the problem?"

"You know we're supposed to be reading *Emma* over the holidays?"

"Are we?" I was starting to wonder whether she'd actually got the right person. Maybe she was getting me muddled with somebody else.

"Yeah. You know, for English next year?"

Dimly, my brain began to register what she was talking about. School work was something I'd put totally on the back burner since the end of term: we hadn't even got our GCSE results yet.

"Blimey, you're keen!"

She laughed. "Not really. I'm just totally bored and I thought hey, I can't possibly be any more fed-up than I am now, let's give *Emma* a whirl."

"Right." I was impressed. Well, kind of. When I'm bored the only reading matter my brain can cope with is trashy teeny romance-type stuff. Jane Austen is for the seriously cerebral moments, in my book (ho ho). "So how can I help?"

For one alarming moment I thought she was going to suggest coming round so we could read it together. But no.

"I think I left my copy round at Jaz's," she told me. (Aha! So probably the unwanted fellow courseworker, then.) "At least, I've looked everywhere for it and I can't find it, and the last time I had it was at Jaz's house just after Mrs Radcliffe gave them out. So I was just wondering – if you're not using yours, could I borrow it? Just till Jaz gets home from holiday and I can get mine back."

"Yeah, sure. I'll dig it out for you." I was pretty sure I knew where my copy was: under my bed, still in my school bag from when they were dished out.

"Brilliant! Shall I come round some time to get it? Or we could meet up in town and have a coffee, maybe?"

"Tell you what." The mention of coffee made me remember Bex. "Are you doing anything on Friday?"

"Friday? Don't think so."

"Why don't you come round here, then? Only I've just met someone who's starting at St Mark's in September, and I've asked her round on Friday afternoon. I was thinking it would be quite nice if she could meet you as well. You know – get to know a few faces before she starts."

"Aw, that's kind of you. Who is she?"

"Her dad's the new vicar at Combe Bridge. She's going to be in the sixth form, like us."

"Oh, right. Yeah, I'm up for that. It must be quite a scary prospect, being new."

Somehow, I couldn't imagine Bex being scared by something as mundane as starting a new school. Stepping alone and unarmed into the lions' enclosure at the zoo, possibly (although by no means definitely);

entering the sixth form at St Mark's, not very likely. Not with her look-at-me dress sense and kick-ass attitude.

"So shall we say about three?"

"Sure."

"Cool. Oh, and Lisa?"

"Yeah?"

"How did you know I was doing English next year?"

I could sense her frowning down the line, trying to recall. "Dunno. Can't remember. I guess Jaz must have told me. See you Friday then, yeah?"

"Hold on! Don't you need to know where I live?"

"Oh, I already know. Brandy Bay, isn't it? That last house on the lane before you get to the cove. Jaz told me that, too."

Chapter Three

Ma chère Mattie!

C'est très beau ici! Et aussi très TRÈS interessant, si tu get what je mean! Il y a un garçon Français ici qui est absolument awesome, il est almost 19, il s'appelle Patrice et il est totalement gorge! Nous sommes going pour un petit drinkie ce soir, so crossez-vous les fingers pour moi!

Tu es mon bestest ami dans le tout monde, et je t'embrasse mille fois!

JAZ xxxxxxxxxxxxxxxx

PS Pardonnez-moi pour les mistakes, mais j'ai lost mon dictionnaire.

It's almost embarrassing to tell you how delighted I was to hear from Jaz. And how spooky was it? She'd been on my mind for much of the previous evening –

I'd not only been missing her, but also wondering how she and Lisa had got so matey without me having known anything about it (well, matey enough to have Lisa round to her house, pass on all the details of where I live and, presumably, give her my phone number), and the very next day here was a postcard from her. It was no substitute for actually having her back home, of course – how could it be? – but it was a sign that she'd been thinking of me, and I was pathetically thrilled when I got downstairs and found the card propped up against the kettle.

On the front was a picture of a romantic-looking little village, all white-painted exteriors and red roofs, nestling amid gently undulating green hills, and all under an impossibly blue sky. Hmm, I thought. Best friend in the whole world I may be, but Jaz had never seen fit to kiss me a thousand times before, even via a postcard. It must be the influence of this French boy, this – I turned the card over again – this *Patrice*.

It wasn't like Jaz to get all gooey about a lad. He must be something special to have her writing that kind of stuff. And in French, too. (Well, OK then, Franglais.) I couldn't help wondering whether she'd got lucky following their "petit drinkie" and got to kiss *him* a thousand times, too. I couldn't wait to find out when she returned home in – I looked at the kitchen calendar – just over two weeks. *Another two weeks! God,*

I thought gloomily. *How am I going to survive that long without being able to tell her all about Mr Buff the Gardener?*

When Lisa turned up on Friday afternoon, on the dot of three, she came bearing gifts.

"It's just a little thank-you," she explained, "for helping me out with *Emma*."

It was a set of three hair slides, one smooth pewter, one a dark polished wood inlaid with brass, and the third covered with a funky Aztec-y print fabric.

"Wow," I said, looking at them sitting on the kitchen table. They looked expensive. I was really touched. "That's really kind of you. There was no need, honestly."

"OK then, I'll have them back." She made a mock lunge towards them and grinned at me. Maybe this afternoon was going to work out OK after all.

Let me explain something about myself. I sometimes seem to have this knack of opening my mouth and saying things without thinking, and it's only later that the possible consequences start to present themselves. Here was a case in point. Ever since inviting Lisa round to meet Bex I'd been having serious misgivings; I mean, what on earth could they possibly have in common, the one a girl I'd never spoken to, whose idea of a fab fun-filled summer afternoon seemed to be sitting reading Jane Austen, and the other, to judge from her appearance at any rate, the Bonsai Rock Chick from Hell? They were bound to hate each other on sight. It would be like a Blue Peter presenter meeting Marilyn Manson; namely, a total disaster, and all because I'd taken it upon myself to act like some kind of one-woman sixth-form friendship agency.

That's what I'd started to think, anyway, but now Lisa had at least showed she had a sense of humour. She was probably going to need it when Bex walked through the door. I thought perhaps I'd better warn her.

"Erm . . . Lisa. There's something you need to know about Bex before she arrives."

She struck a theatrical pose, as if the drama teacher had just told her to do shocked. "What? Don't tell me – she's a mad axe murderer."

"Not quite. She's just, erm, not necessarily what you'd expect from a vicar's daughter." I don't want to come across as being guilty of stereotyping here, but you need to understand just how things are in our neighbourhood. Insular would be one way of putting it. Narrow-minded and stuck in a time warp would be two others. It was little wonder Bex appeared to have scandalized the entire membership of Combe Bridge Mothers' Union. "Look, come on upstairs to my room, and I'll fill you in. My sister's out for the afternoon, so we'll have it to ourselves."

Upstairs, I threw open the bedroom door with a flourish. "Ta da! Welcome to my world. Well, mine and Moll's, at any rate." Kicking off my flip-flops, I vaulted on to my bed and indicated the other – Molly's – with a wave of my arm. "Take a pew."

"Thanks." Lisa sat carefully down on the edge and crossed her legs at the ankles. "This is cool. Really pretty."

She looked round, approvingly, at the overcrowded little room with its odd assortment of pine furniture. The curtains, striped blue and white like a deckchair, fluttered lazily at the open window. Mum had cut them down from a much larger pair she'd bought in a charity shop when Molly gave up her old room to accommodate Rupert and moved in with me. On the desk sat a large bunch of sweet peas that Molly had picked from the garden that morning and shoved haphazardly into a blue and white Cornishware jug. Molly's flotilla of stuffed animals – which she showed no signs of growing out of – were lined up across her pillow, staring fixedly into the middle distance with lolling heads and glassy eyes.

Rather like the way I was regarding Lisa now. In all the time we'd lived in the cottage, none of the friends I'd invited back had ever called the room pretty before. In fact, I couldn't recall anybody even commenting on it.

"Is it? It's just a bedroom. It's not really big enough to share. We're always arguing about whose turn it is to use the desk. But we don't have much choice, seeing as there's five of us living here and only three bedrooms."

"It must be so nice to have a sister to share with." Lisa's eyes stopped roaming round the room and met mine. She smiled. "I've always wanted that."

I laughed. "You can have my sister if you like. On permanent loan. You come and share this room with her and I'll go and live at yours instead!"

"No, I'm serious. I really would love a sister." She clasped her hands between her knees and leant forward eagerly. "So come on, then. What's all this about Bex?"

"Well. . ." How to explain in a way that wouldn't sound off-putting, or just plain bitchy? "Like I said, she's not exactly what you'd expect a vicar's daughter to be like."

"You mean she doesn't carry a bible around and sing hymns while accompanying herself on the piano?" Lisa giggled.

"Shouldn't think so, no. Nu-metal on the bass guitar, possibly. Hymns on the piano, unlikely."

"Yeah?" Lisa sat up, her eyes widening. "Is she a punk?"

"Not really. More, like, grungy. You know, rock-chick kit, chains, tattoos—"

"*Yeah?*" She sat up even straighter. "Cool!"

"Well, one tattoo," I amended. "That I could see. And she swears like a squaddie. But she seems really nice."

I started to recount Bex's tales about her encounters with all the Mrs Cakes of the parish, when the room was suddenly filled with the unusual sound of a car going by. I say unusual because our house is at the very end of a steep, narrow, muddy track that terminates in a set of equally steep, muddy etc. steps, leading directly on to the beach. Next stop, the Atlantic. The top end of the lane is festooned with signs of the Private/No Entry/Dead End variety, helpfully provided by the council after a succession of cars came to grief near (or, in one memorable case, halfway down) the beach steps during the first summer after we moved in and before our drive was widened. Every so often some brave or foolhardy soul will still venture down, but once they approach our cottage and realize that the signs weren't in fact lying, they then do a rapid about-turn in our drive.

Today, though, I could tell from the engine note that the car in question had gone straight past. I got to my feet and stuck my head out of the window. Sure enough, a rather battered old dark blue Golf had come to a standstill a few metres past the drive and was sat, engine throbbing, while the driver presumably tried to work out what to do next.

I tutted, and withdrew my head. "Another grockle," I pronounced. "Honestly, I can never work out whether they can't read, or are just . . . oh, hang on! It's Bex!"

She had thrown the passenger door open and leapt out, slamming the door shut with a bang. As she bent to speak through the open window to the driver, I stuck my head out through the bedroom one again.

"Bex! Hey, Bex!" I waved at her as she straightened up and turned round, a puzzled look on her face. The she glanced up and saw me. "I'll come down and open the gate – the GATE!" I yelled, leaning out as far as I dared, and stabbing the air with a forefinger in the general direction of our front drive. "He can reverse up then, and turn round so he's pointing in the right. . . Oh, never mind! Hang on, I'm coming downstairs!"

And I shot down the stairs and out of the front door.

"Hi, Mattie!" Bex, dressed all in black, was standing by the gate. She grinned at me as I picked my way, barefooted, down the drive. I'd been in so much of a hurry I'd left my flip-flops on the bedroom floor where I'd kicked them off earlier.

"Here you go, I'll just open this and then your dad can—oww, oww!" I trod slap-bang on a mussel shell, dropped by some seagull, and had to hop the rest of the way to the gate.

"Aw, thanks, hon." Bex stood in the lane and windmilled her arms at the car, which obligingly reversed at top speed towards the open gate. Unfortunately, I was still standing there bent over my injured foot, examining it for traces of shell.

"Hang on a tick!" Alarmed, I hobbled out of the way in the nick of time as Bex's dad shot backwards up the drive, missing me by inches.

Only it wasn't Bex's dad.

"Oh my God!" A face poked out of the driver's window. A fairly aghast face. A fairly aghast *familiar* face. It was none other than Mr Buff the Gardener. "Christ, I'm so sorry! I didn't see you there. Are you OK?"

"Um. . ." I'd like to say that it was on the tip of my tongue to say no, actually, I'm not OK, I've got a shell in my foot and you nearly ran me over, so how about getting out of that car and coming over to where I can see you properly and apologizing some more. . . Only of course it wasn't. There was nothing on the tip of my tongue other than saliva (drool, I mean – Lordy, he was *gorgeous*. . .), and I just stood and kind of simpered at him until Bex banged on the bonnet with the flat of her hand, making us both jump.

"Gabe!" she yelled. "You prat and a half! Mattie's the only person in this dump who's been nice to me, and you practically flatten her! You'd better go before you do any more damage."

He rolled his eyes at me cheerfully and mouthed "Sorry." Then he withdrew his head back inside, took the car out of reverse with a crunching of gears, exchanged a couple of inaudible words through the still-open window with Bex, and was gone, filling the lane with the smell of hot exhaust.

Bex tutted. "I'm so sorry about him," she said, striding up the drive towards the front door. "I sometimes think he's not safe to be let out alone. I saw the danger signs at the top of the lane and I did warn him. I told him to go slowly, but oh no, he's the demon driver, isn't he? He's the – what?" She stopped suddenly, and looked at us both, looking at her. Lisa had followed me down the stairs and now stood open-mouthed in the doorway as she took in Bex, dressed on this sweltering summer's afternoon in head-to-toe unremitting black, topped off with a piece of black lace tied in a bow on top of her head and, round her neck, a studded dog's collar that looked uncannily like the real thing (which I guess was quite appropriate. Vicar's daughter, dog collars, blah blah blah. Ha ha ha).

I suddenly realized that my face mirrored Lisa's. Not because of Bex – I'd been expecting her to be dressed unconventionally, in fact I'd have been disappointed if she hadn't been – but at this totally unexpected re-sighting of Mr Buff.

"Blimey, Bex," I said, with an isn't-it-funny little laugh to cover up my fly-catching expression. "Nice work getting your dad's gardener to drive you over!"

She frowned. "Sorry?"

"He's a bit tasty though, isn't he? I bet you spend all your time hanging out of the window trying to catch a glimpse of him weeding the flowerbeds. Or sunbathing on the lawn while he's mowing it. Phwoar! I wouldn't mind him mowing my—"

"Oh, you mean *Gabriel*!" She spoke his name, his beautiful angelic name, with such dismissive scorn I should have instantly realized that I'd yet again jumped to the wrong conclusions and was left standing with my foot jammed firmly in my mouth. "Gardener be buggered. He's my brother."

"It'll end in tears," Molly pronounced, later that evening. It had been well past six o'clock when she got home from Chloë's and found Lisa and me still closeted upstairs in the bedroom. Bex was long gone, collected shortly after five not, disappointingly, by her brother, but by her father, who drew up in a small, immaculately clean car that he turned neatly round in the drive without having to be told, and sat patiently in while he waited for Bex to come out. As soon as I saw him again, I knew who it was he'd reminded me of when Moll and I had met him the other day. Not

Geoffrey, but his own son, who I'd seen just moments earlier. The height, the build, the colouring, even the smile. . . It was the family resemblance I'd spotted. I just hadn't realized it.

Bex's departure couldn't have been more different from her arrival, and as soon as she'd gone Lisa and I turned breathlessly to each other and started talking non-stop. It was about Bex to begin with – her look, her attitude, her sheer *out-there*ness – but it wasn't long before our discussion turned to the flawless speciman of total hot-ness that was her brother Gabriel. Which is how Moll found us when she came in.

"Oh, hi," she'd said, smiling in a friendly fashion. She's much nicer to my mates than I am to hers, is Moll. I'm inclined to throw a proper wobbly if I find her friends in our room when I'm not expecting them to be there. It feels like they're invading my territory. Moll doesn't appear to have the same problem with it, though. "You must be Bex," she said, and smiled again.

"Er, no," said Lisa, smiling back. "She had to go. I'm Lisa. Lisa Gray: Jaz's friend from St Mark's?"

The vague thought floated into my brain that Lisa was somehow being promoted from Jaz's erstwhile geography coursework partner to full-on friend, but it floated right out again when Moll took herself back downstairs and left us to it. Why is exclaiming and swooning with somebody else similarly like-minded over a particularly fine example of lad-hood such a blast? Maybe on this occasion, though, it was partly because I hadn't remotely fancied anyone for ages, and it was reassuring to discover all my lusting-after equipment was still in full working order.

But Molly wasn't interested in any of that. "It'll end in tears."

I blinked at her. "What d'you mean, tears? How?"

"I heard what you were saying about that boy. Honestly, Mat – what are you like? It was, like, totally gross! I heard you and wotshername giggling about him."

Giggling indeed! The trouble with my little sister is she has no respect for her elders. Well, none for me, at any rate. Attack seemed the best form of defence, although I did wonder what exactly she'd overheard.

"You shouldn't have been eavesdropping, then, should you?"

"I couldn't help it! I could hear you two at the bottom of the stairs, going on about the size of his—"

"OK, OK, no need to get all graphic." Obvious what she'd overheard, then. I coughed, embarrassed. I hadn't realized we were being so loud. "We were only having a laugh. How can that end in tears?"

"If he's as good-looking as that, he'll know it," she pronounced, with all the experienced wisdom of her not-quite-fourteen years. "That kind of lad always does. Remember Sam Barker?"

Ah. Sam Barker. What can I tell you about him? Two words are all it really needs: Player and Loser. (Although Bastard would fit the bill pretty well, too.) He came, he saw, he conquered . . . almost. Luckily for me, I came to my senses in time. But only just. He was the reason I hadn't fancied anyone for so long. I'd gone right off romance since he and I went spectacularly belly-up earlier in the year.

I groaned. "Cheers, Moll. Thanks for reminding me."

"You know I'm right. Who were you talking about, anyway? Anyone I know?"

"Well, yes, actually. Now you come to mention it. You remember Lawnmower Man? At the vicarage the other day? Well, it turns out he's not the gardener at all. He's Bex's brother."

Molly's eyes widened to the size of saucers. "No way!"

"Yes way. And there's more."

"Don't tell me. Bex has suddenly become your best friend. Yours and, er, Lisa's."

"Not quite." I pouted. Was I that obvious?

"So, what? C'mon Mat – spill!"

"Well . . . she's asked us round next week. Me and Lisa."

"Ha!" Molly crowed. "I knew it! She's got a fit brother, so you're going to live round there for the rest of the holidays! It'll end in tears, Mattie – you mark my words!" she said, wagging a mock Old

Granny-type finger at me, and I tutted and rolled my eyes at her and thought, *Little sisters, eh? What do they know?*

Oh boy. If only I'd listened to her.

Chapter Four

When Mum and Geoffrey were first married, I thought my world had come to an end. That's not just me being melodramatic, it's the plain truth. I'm not saying *the* world, mind, I'm saying *my* world. And to be fair, the world as I knew it actually did end the day the pair of them strolled hand in hand down the makeshift aisle between two banks of chairs in the flower-bedecked hotel room where their wedding was held, and out into the dewy-eyed perfect sunset that was their life together. . .

Only it wasn't, of course. Their life, I mean. Because where Mum and Geoffrey went, the rest of us came too: Molly and Rupert and me. And there, in a nutshell, was the rub. I thought I'd never get over there being five of us instead of three, the encroaching of these almost-strangers upon my life, the enforced sharing of things – my room, my space, my *mother* for heaven's sake – that had once been mine.

I thought I'd never get used to it. But of course I did,

or I at least began to, bit by bit. I'm not going to pretend it was easy – life's not like that, all nice and neat and tidy – but as time went by, it did what time can usually be relied upon to do and gradually turned the unpleasant and unusual into the ordinary. In short, I got used to it. Which isn't to say everything in the garden suddenly got rosy: Geoffrey had always been just about bearable, OK-ish, in a nerdy Professor Boff kind of way, but Rupert remained – well, Rupert. What can I say? Even now, I can't ever see me looking at him and thinking, yeah mate, you definitely come from Planet Normal, but hey. We both make an effort. Most of the time.

Which is, I guess, my way of explaining what prompted me to do what I'm about to relate: I was trying to make an effort.

A week or so after Bex and Lisa had come round, Mum and Geoffrey were on a rare night out at the cinema – although in typical Mum-and-Geoffrey fashion it wasn't the latest Hollywood blockbuster but some arty Japanese film with subtitles at the arts centre in Luscombe – and Molly and Rupert had long since retired to their respective beddy-byes. I'd have been ditto, only I'd started watching some reality show crapola on TV, and fallen asleep on the sitting-room sofa. I came round with a start to see it was getting on for midnight, and no sign of Mum and Geoffrey. *Wow,*

I thought, *it must have been a good film. Or perhaps just a long one. Or – I know – they fell asleep, like me, and are still there.* . . . I wasn't remotely worried about them. Luscombe's only a half-hour drive away, and Geoffrey is possibly the safest driver in the world. Possibly the slowest, too, but nobody can accuse him of being reckless.

Amused by the notion of the two of them snoozing away in the arts centre auditorium (but knowing the more plausible reason for their lateness was that they'd gone for something to eat afterwards), I turned off the TV and lights and went into the darkened kitchen, rubbing my eyes and yawning, in search of a drink of water. I'd only just reached in the cupboard for a glass when I heard a key in the front door, followed by the bizarre but unmistakable sound of my mother and Geoffrey whispering and giggling together out in the hallway. I kid you not – *giggling*. It's not completely unknown for Mum to giggle after imbibing too much alcohol (in her case, about half a glass), but I knew there was no way on earth that Geoffrey would drink anything if he was driving. Even so, there he was, tittering like a good 'un. It was like overhearing Saddam Hussein warbling a chorus of "We Wish You a Merry Christmas". It was oddly disturbing. I felt caught out, embarrassed, like they'd arrived home while I was doing something I shouldn't be. My hand, halfway to the cupboard, froze in shock, and I sent up a silent prayer of thanks that I hadn't switched the kitchen lights on.

Not that it would have mattered if I had. Oblivious of anything or anybody else, the giggling (joined now by a low murmuring of the "mmm" variety) moved from the hallway to the sitting room. Fascinated, I crept out of the kitchen and peeped through the open door of the sitting room. There was just enough light in the room – it was a cloudless, moonlit night – for me to make out Mum and Geoffrey entwined together on the sofa, indulging in a spot of . . . well, sorry if this shocks you, gentle reader, but in what can only be described as *snogging*.

Amused, appalled and alarmed in equal measure, I stood rooted to the spot in the doorway. I didn't mean to spy on them, but I couldn't seem to move. Besides, if I attempted to go past the door and upstairs, you could bet your life I'd disturb them by stepping on one of the creaky stairs or the noisy floorboards on the landing, and how would I explain that away? They'd be totally mortified if they realized I'd seen them in the throes of passion. More to the point, so would I.

After a mercifully short while they came up for air, and Mum gave a great gusty sigh.

"It's a lovely idea," she said, as if there'd been no

break in their previous unheard-by-me conversation, "but I just don't think it would work."

"I don't see why not," said Geoffrey gently. "Surely they're old enough to understand how significant it is? I don't think one weekend away together in an entire year is too much to ask for."

"I don't know." Mum sounded dubious. "Remember how they were about the actual wedding?"

"As I recall, they were fine about the actual wedding. The problems came later."

"I know. That's what I mean. It's still early days – I just don't think we should rock the boat. I'd never forgive myself if we went away for a lovely romantic anniversary weekend – and it *does* sound lovely and romantic, darling, don't get me wrong – and then got home to find they'd been fighting non-stop."

"I really don't think they would," Geoffrey said stoutly. "I think things have come on enormously in the past few months. I really think we should give them the benefit of the doubt."

"Maybe." Mum didn't sound convinced. "But you know how Mattie can be."

A moment's silence. Then, "It's not just Mattie," said Geoffrey. "Rupert's been far from blameless. Anyway, it's late. Let's talk about it again in the morning, shall we?"

"If you like. But I don't think there's much—"

"In the morning, Alice," he repeated, with more

firmness than I knew he possessed. "Now then." He got up from the sofa and I ducked back, out of sight. "I just want to catch the weather forecast. Why don't you go on up?"

"No, that's all right. I'll wait for you. I'll make some tea, shall I?"

The room was filled with an unearthly flickering glow as Geoffrey switched on the television, and it's a measure of how much things had changed that I didn't announce my presence by making a scene, pretending to vomit at the prospect of them going away for a romantic weekend, or protesting loudly that Mum had dared suggest the past aggro had all been caused by me. (Or perhaps it just showed that, astonishingly, I'd actually grown up a bit.) Whatever: I didn't do any of those things. Instead, I fled upstairs as quickly as I could, and to hell with the creaky stairs, before Mum could come out to put the kettle on and find me still standing there.

The next morning, I woke Molly at the crack of dawn.

"Wha – wha? Whassgoinon?" she demanded, thrashing around under her duvet and acting as panicked as if we were on board the *Titanic* and I'd just informed her that a bloody great lump of ice had found its way on to the deck.

"Family conference," I told her briskly. "Come on – get your dressing gown. We're going in."

"Going in where?"

"Into the Lair of the Rupert."

He was already up and dressed, and sitting (predictably) at his computer. His bed was neatly made, the pillow placed just so, the duvet smooth and unwrinkled.

"Blimey," I exclaimed, "didn't you go to bed last night?"

He turned from his desk and took in the sight of Molly and me standing bedraggled, pyjama-clad and yawning, in his doorway. Then he looked pointedly at the clock on the desk. The hands stood at ten past nine. (OK, I know I said it was the crack of dawn, but come on – ten past nine *is* the crack of dawn in the summer holidays. . .)

Clearly not for Rupert, though. He blinked at us, slowly, in that curious, heavy-lidded, lizard-like manner of his.

"Of course I did," he said, at last. "I've been up since half-past seven. I've always been an early wiser."

"Aah," I said, sagely. Next to me, Molly stifled a snigger that she turned into a cough.

"I always twy and wite my blog first thing," he went on earnestly. "And then there's the weather weports to fill in, and stuff like that."

"Right," I agreed. I didn't have a clue what he was on about.

"So." He swung round on his swivel chair to face us, rubbing his hands together in a carbon copy of his father's habit. It was like looking at a mini-Geoffrey. Weird. "How can I help you?"

For a moment I forgot what we'd come in for. I stood and stared at him like a loony for a good ten seconds before his pet rat, Colin, started running on the exercise wheel in his cage with a sudden clatter, and my brain clicked into gear.

"Have you two realized," I began slowly, looking at Rupert and Molly in turn, "that it's Mum and Geoffrey's wedding anniversary in a couple of weeks?"

Briefly, I filled them in on what I'd overheard the previous night, which basically boiled down to a) anniversary, b) proposed weekend away and c) concern about the three of us tearing each other to shreds in their absence. (I left out the preliminary giggling and snogging – there is such a thing as too much information.)

When I'd finished, Rupert nodded. "Hmm," he said. "So they want to go away to celebwate? Well, I think they should go. I think they deserve a tweat."

I looked at him with a new respect (only a teensy-weensy bit, though. He was still a dweeb).

"Cool," I said. "That's what I thought, too."

"So how can we persuade them that we can be twusted by ourselves?"

"Leave that to me," I declared. "I have a cunning plan."

Molly scratched her armpit and yawned. "Sorted. Can I go back to bed now?"

OK, I admit it. I did have a slight ulterior motive. Nothing sinister, nothing underhand – just that, well, if Mum and Geoffrey were going to be away for a weekend, I'd be able to have some friends over, wouldn't I? Just one or two. Jaz, obviously. Her birthday had been and gone while she was away in France, so we hadn't been able to celebrate it together as we usually did. And a couple of others from school. And Lisa – oh, and maybe Bex: it would be the ideal way for her to get to know some more people from St Mark's. (And, you know, if her brother happened to be free too, then the more the merrier. Not that I'd actually invite him, as such. That would be way too forward.) And the weekend in question was around the time of the GCSE results. Celebrate or commiserate, we could see them in in style.

I mentioned it to Lisa and Bex that afternoon, at our return fixture round at the vicarage.

"My mum and stepfather might be going away for the weekend in a couple of weeks," I started casually. "It's their first wedding anniversary."

"Aw," said Lisa. "Bless! How romantic is that?"

"So I thought you might like to come round. It's not definite at the moment, but—"

"Yay!" Bex high-fived the air. "Partaaay!" Then she laughed. "Your face! Don't worry, hon. I'm only kidding. It doesn't have to be a party. An evening in with some DVDs and a takeaway would be cool. Listen, do either of you want something to drink? I'm parched."

I didn't have the heart to tell her that we don't have a DVD player, only a video (which is so old you practically have to wind it up to get it working), and that the nearest takeaway is fifteen miles away – besides which, nobody delivers out to Brandy Bay. Our house isn't what you'd call over-blessed with the accoutrements of modern-day living.

Bex went to get drinks, and I was just taking a sneaky peek round the sitting room, knowing Mum would never forgive me if I went home without being able to tell her all about the vicarage's interior design details, when an overexcited black Labrador charged in through the open French windows, followed closely by none other than – yup, you've guessed. The vision of loveliness that was Bex's brother Gabriel, clad in floppy beige linen-y trousers and a white shirt that was unbuttoned and showed off his smooth butterscotch-coloured chest to mouthwatering perfection.

"Badger," he yelled. "Give it back, you total—" Then

he caught sight of us: me, lurking by the fireplace with a china ballerina in my hand, and Lisa, who was staring adoringly at him.

"Umm. . ." I said intelligently, and hastily replaced the ornament on the mantelpiece.

"Oh, hi," Gabriel said. "I didn't know Bex had visitors. *Badger!*"

The dog had a large brown mule-type sandal clamped between its grinning jaws, and was wandering around the room showing it proudly to Lisa and me and wagging from the shoulders down. Gabriel made a lunge at him. The dog sidestepped nimbly and continued to wag.

"He thinks he's being funny," Gabriel remarked. I was trying to think of some witty and incisive response to this, something that would etch me for ever into his brain as "that clever and amusing friend of my sister's" (yeah, right. . .) when the door opened and in came Bex herself. She was carrying a large wooden tray, heaped with glasses and plates of cake and biscuits, and a tall frosted jug of orange juice that clinked gently with ice cubes.

She placed the tray down on a handy side table and tutted. "You'll never get him to hand stuff over if you chase him and yell. He just thinks you're playing. Badger – *sit!*" She pointed a stern forefinger at the dog, and to our surprise the dog obeyed her. "Now then –

drop. *Drop!*" Bex removed the shoe from his mouth and handed it to her brother, who grinned amiably.

"Aw, thanks, Sis. You're a star. Scary, but still a star." Then he examined the shoe more closely and the grin faded. "The bugger! He's put teeth marks all over it!"

Bex shrugged, unconcerned. "Serves you right for leaving it lying around. You know what he's like with shoes." She handed me a plate of cake and started to pour orange juice into the glasses. Gabriel reached past her and took a slice of chocolate cake, cramming it into his mouth.

"Mmm," he said indistinctly through the crumbs. "S'good. Who made this one?"

"Me, as it happens. And it's not for you, it's for Mattie and Lisa."

"What, you mean all this is for you three? You'll turn into a right bunch of heifers if you polish off this lot. I think you need a helping hand!" He grinned again and picked up a handful of chocolate biscuits.

Bex curled her upper lip at him.

"Please ignore my brother," she told us. "Most people do. Anyway, he's just going."

Cramming the biscuits into his mouth, Gabriel sighed in a put-upon manner, then whistled for the dog and turned to go. Just before he went out through the French windows he looked over his shoulder, and winked at us behind Bex's back. Badger took advantage of this lapse in concentration, snatched a small embroidered cushion off the sofa and legged it outside, with Gabriel in hot pursuit.

"Badger! *Badger!*"

As he disappeared across the back lawn Lisa let out a huge sigh, as if she'd been holding her breath for a long time. Perhaps she had been.

"Bex," she said, dreamily, "he is just *gorgeous!*"

"He is quite cute, isn't he? He's not very well trained, though. He's always running off with stuff he's not supposed to have."

Lisa giggled and put her hand in front of her mouth. "Not the dog! I meant your brother!"

Bex handed me a glass, and her eyes met mine over the top of it. "Oh, right," she said, deadpan.

"She has got a point," I said, taking the glass. "He is lushness squared."

Lisa squealed. "Hands off, Mattie! I saw him first! Anyway, what would *Andy* say?"

She said the name so archly that I didn't get to contradict her and say, actually you're wrong, I saw Gabriel first, days ago.

"Who's Andy?" Bex asked.

"Just a guy at school." I turned to Lisa. "I don't get what you mean. Why should Andy say anything?"

"Aren't you two an item? I just thought he probably wouldn't like you drooling over somebody else."

I felt the blood rush to my face. Heaven knows why I was blushing. Unless it wasn't embarrassment but annoyance, something to do with the fact that Lisa didn't think to mention Andy the other day when we were closeted in my room, lusting together over Gabriel.

"We are so not an item," I responded hotly. "Where did you get that idea from?"

Lisa put out a hand to take a biscuit, then changed her mind and let it fall. "Only because somebody told me you were together after you split up with Sam Barker."

"Well, we're not. We're mates, that's all. I haven't seen him once these holidays. I haven't even spoken to him."

"It's all right, Mattie. I believe you." She gave a nonchalant shrug, and smiled at Bex. "So come on then. Give us the low-down."

"The low-down on what?"

"On your brother, of course! How old is he? What's he do? Is he going to St Mark's too?"

"And more importantly, has he got a girlfriend?" I finished for her. These were exactly the questions that had been going round in my brain since he was revealed as Bex's brother, and not the gardener after all.

"He's nineteen and he works at McDonald's, so no. He's not going to be at St Mark's." Bex flopped down in the nearest chair, crossed her legs and took a large swig of juice.

"McDonald's? What a waste!" Lisa squealed. "He should be a model, looking like that!"

"Or a Chippendale," I put in.

Bex gave us a funny look. "Riiiight. . ."

"No, really," Lisa insisted. "I mean it. I bet he gets loads of customers coming in, just to see him!"

"He's not going to be there for long. Only until the New Year, then he's going to France to be a ski instructor. He's on a gap year," Bex told us. "He's off to uni after that."

"Really? Where's he going?" I asked.

"Depends on his A levels." Bex's foot began to tap in mid-air.

"What's he going to do?"

"French and Italian." That explained the Proust. Bex suddenly jumped to her feet. "Right, that's it. That's your lot."

Startled, we both stared at her. "What d'you mean?" I asked.

"The third degree. Have you any *idea* –" She poured herself another drink, clumsily slopping the juice over the sides of the glass on to the tray "– how sick I get of it?"

Our staring intensified. "Of what?" I ventured timidly.

Glass in hand, she glared at us for a moment or two before her face softened and she sat down again. "Of people asking me about my brother. *Fancying* him," she said with scorn.

A moment's silence. Why hadn't I realized, picked up on her irritation with our questions about him?

Timidly, I said, "I expect you must get fed-up with it."

"You could say that, yeah." She looked at us then, and gave us a sudden, rueful smile. "But hey. Not your fault. Every so often I go off on one about it. Just ignore me."

"It must be tough," Lisa sympathized. "But you do know it's *you* we want to be friends with, don't you? It's got nothing to do with your brother."

I knew Lisa meant to be reassuring, but it seemed to me she was just making matters worse. Truth to tell, I really liked Bex, and wanted to be friends with her for her own sake. I wasn't yet certain of Lisa's motivation, but if she was only being nice to Bex because of her brother, I didn't want to be lumped in the same bracket. How cringe-making would that be? Hurriedly, I changed the subject.

"Tell you what," I said. "That chocolate cake's fab. Can I have another piece?"

Chapter Five

Yay! Jaz is back!!

> *AND – I can hardly believe it, but it's true – Mum and Geoffy Baby are definitely going away for the weekend to celebrate their anniversary!!!*
>
> *AND AND AND!!!! I asked Mum if I could have some friends round on the Saturday, and she said I don't see why not!!!!!!!! (Which pretty much amounts to agreeing to a party, doesn't it. . .?)*
>
> *I can't believe my life is actually being this good for once! YAYNESS!!!*
>
> *Wonder if Gabriel would come along, if I asked him. . .?*

By far the best thing, though, was Jaz being back. She came round straight after lunch, and we went down to the cove for some privacy (far too many flapping ears in my house these days). The first thing I told her about was Mum and Geoffrey's weekend away.

"A party? Seriously?" Jaz, sitting next to me on a

large flat rock at the top end of the beach, looked satisfyingly impressed.

"Seriously. Although not a huge one. I mean, my place just isn't big enough." Plus Mum's tolerance levels probably weren't that high. I didn't say that, though.

"Hey, don't knock it. A party's a party."

"True. And at least it'll get Mum and Geoffrey out of the house. They've been wafting round recently like a pair of fourteen year olds. Sickening. I keep feeling like telling them to get a room."

Jaz sniggered. "Isn't it *sooo* embarrassing when parents get snuggly with each other? Almost as bad as when they try to dance. So, who're you going to invite to this party, then?"

It was an important question. I considered it, looking round the beach at the assorted visitors doing tourist-y things (swimming, sunbathing, digging, or, in the case of two small irritating boys close to us, running around waving large plastic swords and yelling their heads off).

I tutted loudly. "Why can't some parents supervise their kids properly?"

"I know. Pain in the bum isn't the word." Jaz sighed, and arranged her long, elegant limbs across the rock, the better to catch the sun's rays. It was an incredibly hot afternoon – ANOTHER SCORCHER!, as certain tabloids were plastering across their front pages day after day. According to them, there was nothing else of much importance going on in the world apart from the UK heatwave.

"No. It's four words." It was hardly Comedy Store material, but Jaz snorted down her nose as amused as if I'd come up with some original witty epigram.

"You know what, Mat? I so missed you in France. I really wished you could have been there too."

"Yeah, well, I missed you too," I muttered. Jaz and me have never had that touchy-feely, I-wuv-you-you're-my-bestest-friend-in-da-whole-wide-world type relationship. Doesn't mean we don't care about each other, it was just unusual for her to come over all emotional on me. I didn't quite know how to respond. I scooped up a handful of sand and let the grains trickle through my fingers.

"I kept saying to Patrice, Mattie would have so loved all this," she said.

I smirked. "Didn't know you were into threesomes. Wouldn't I have been a bit – you know – *de trop*?" I was dead proud of myself for dredging up a bit of French from my thankfully long-past GCSE, but it went right over Jaz's head. The beloved's name had been mentioned anew – she'd already spent two hours on the phone last night telling me all about him, and another hour this morning – and she was off on one again.

"He was so – you know – *sympathique*." She gave a big, heartfelt sigh. "I've never met anyone like him before. Why are French guys so damn *sexy*?"

"Dunno. Something to do with the accent, I guess. *Eh, chérie – voulez-vous couchez avec moi ce soir?*" I was well into Frog mode now, but Jaz wasn't impressed. She turned and clouted me on the arm, pouting.

"Don't mock! You'll be laughing on the other side of your face when he comes over here to see me."

"I'd be amazed, not laughing. C'mon, Jaz – it was just a holiday romance, right?"

"Wrong." With a look of triumph, she fished her tiny mobile out of the equally tiny purse-on-a-string she wore round her neck. "I've not been back twenty-four hours yet and he's already sent me three texts, look!" She fiddled with the phone, then grinned. "Oops. Best not read that one, it's a bit – erm – fruity! Well, basically, he's saying he might be coming over here in the Christmas holidays, and if he does he wants us to meet up."

I picked up another handful of sand. "Cool. That'll be nice, won't it?"

"Nice doesn't even come close. Just you wait till you see him, Mat – you won't be able to believe your eyes, I'm telling you! His smile is just the most. . ." She trailed off. "I'm going on about him, aren't I?"

"No, no, that's fine." I waved an airy hand and

settled back on the rock. "You carry on. I'll just do a spot of sunbathing while you describe his smile again. It's not a problem, honestly."

"Yeah, it is. I'm getting boring." She was contrite. "You were telling me about your party. Who did you say was coming?"

"I didn't. But, well, you, obviously. And the usual crowd. Oh, and Lisa, I guess. Seeing as you two are such big buddies."

"Lisa?" She frowned. "Which one? I know at least three Lisas."

"Lisa Gray? The one you did your geography coursework with last term?"

"Oh, right. We're not big buddies, though. What makes you say that?"

I pursed my lips, musing. "Not sure. Just the impression she gave me."

"And she gave you this impression when?" Jaz looked puzzled.

"She came round – she wanted to borrow a book. I've seen her a couple of times while you were away." Trailing an arm beside the rock, I scooped up more sand.

"And she told you we were big buddies?" She looked even more puzzled. "Weird."

"No, she didn't say that exactly. Just. . ." Just what? What had Lisa said that had made me think that? I couldn't remember. Not only that, it seemed unimportant now. Now my own big buddy was back on the scene. I waved my sand-less hand. "It's no big deal. I must have just got hold of the wrong end of the stick. So, are you up for this do, or what?"

"You bet! You should know me by know – always ready to partay! Hey!" Jaz leant towards me conspiratorially. "You'll be asking Andy, won't you?"

"Noooo!" I wailed, chucking the sand down. "Not you as well! Why does everybody think Andy and me are together?"

"Woah! Chill! Did I say I thought you were together?"

"Well, no. But you kind of implied it."

"No, I didn't. I just asked if you'll be asking him. Look, Mat, it's so obvious he fancies you, I just wondered if you might – you know – take the opportunity for a bit of *lurve* action."

"I don't want a bit of *lurve* action, thanks. I went right off all that after Sam. I thought you understood."

"Well, yeah, I do. Totally. But you can't hide yourself away for ever. You know what they say – you gotta get back on the horse."

It was typical Jaz; she was all loved up herself, so she thought everybody else wanted to be, too. The truth was, Andy and I were just friends, despite what other people might think. An erstwhile mate of Sam's, Andy had made it plain what he'd thought of the way Sam had treated me, and had been a total honey to me. But I absolutely didn't fancy him, and regardless of Jaz's comment I was pretty sure he didn't feel like that about me, either. In fact, the whole topic was beginning to make me feel uncomfortable. But there was one sure-fire way to get her off the subject. . .

"Actually, now you come to mention it, there is someone I wouldn't mind getting back on the horse with. It's not Andy, though."

As I suspected, all thoughts of me and Andy dissolved as I told her about my encounters to date with Gabriel Foxcroft, no holds barred. It was, I admit, quite satisfying to be able to tell her that, while she'd been dallying with Patrice, I'd been eying up some totty of my own (well, perhaps not my *own*, not exactly, but get him to my party and who knows. . .?).

"And you say his sister's going to St Mark's in September?" Jaz asked, clearly intrigued.

The two sword-wielding little horrors dashed past us, shrieking, and I pulled an evil face at them.

"Yup. Into the sixth form, same as us. She's way cool – St Mark's isn't going to know what's hit it, I can tell you." The boys screeched to a standstill right in front of us, and stuck their tongues out. "How delightful. Tell you what, Jaz, seeing as this beach experience is going majorly downhill, how d'you fancy a little expedition?"

We got off the bus just up the road from the church, and as we walked past it the sound of peaceful organ music drifted gently through the sultry August air. I imagined Bex up in her room in the adjacent vicarage, playing thrash rock or nu-punk or whatever music she was into at an ear-bleedingly high volume, and observed again what a contrast she was to her father's nice, middle-class, conservative lifestyle. You didn't have to be a psychologist to figure out that was at least partly why she behaved the way she did, but it was little surprise the two of them didn't get on.

We opened the front gate of the vicarage – no sign of Gabriel doing his shirtless Alan Titchmarsh bit today, sadly – and walked up the garden path to the door.

"Don't react to how Bex looks when you see her," I told Jaz as I rang the doorbell. "God knows what she'll be wearing, but it's bound to be, erm, controversial. She's actually really nice, very friendly and all that, so if you just act like you're quite used to seeing people dressed in black bin bags and safety pins, or whatever get-up she's in today, it'll be. . ."

I trailed off as, through the Victorian stained glass set into the front door, we could see the dim shape of a small figure moving up the hallway towards us. Next to

74

me, Jaz composed her features, mentally preparing herself to meet Bex as she opened the door.

Only it wasn't Bex. It was an elderly woman with a neat grey perm and an apron. The cleaner, or the housekeeper. Something like that. She smiled at us.

"Oh!" I exclaimed, my greeting and introductory whatnot dying on my lips.

"Can I help you?" the woman asked us, in a friendly way. "I'm afraid the vicar's not in."

"Oh, no," I assured her hastily. "That's OK. We didn't want him." Did Jaz and me really look like the sort of people who come calling on the vicar, I wondered? Bit of a blow to the self-image, that. "We've come to see Bex. Rebecca. His daughter."

"Aaah." She nodded. "Friends of hers, are you?"

"She's in the same year as us at school. Or she's going to be, next term."

"Aaah," she said again, and took a step further towards us. "'Fraid she's not in, my love. But funnily enough, another young girl called round earlier to see her. She seems very popular already, given they've only just moved here." She gave us another smile. "This other girl said the same as you, that they're both going to be in the sixth form together. You'd probably know her."

Unless word about Bex's newbie status had got out round more of St Mark's future sixth-formers, there weren't a lot of people who'd fit the bill. Jaz and I exchanged glances.

"I think we probably do," I said. "What did she look like, this other girl?"

"Ooh, let me think now. Do you know, I can hardly remember, isn't that odd?"

"Did she have kind of straight, brownish hair and . . . erm. . ." Try as I might, I couldn't think of any more of Lisa's distinguishing features.

But it hardly mattered, since Mrs Cleaner was nodding. "That's right. And a big round face. Happy-looking girl, she was."

"So did they go out somewhere together, do you know?"

"No, my love. Rebecca's out, like her dad. But this girl seemed to know young Gabriel. Rebecca's brother, you know? She went off to the church with him. He's not come back yet, so I think they're most likely still there if you want to go over and find her."

The organ music had changed from the soft pastoral strains we'd heard floating through the air as we'd walked past, to some thunderous full-on piece that filled the building with a deafening wall of sound. As Jaz and I walked up the aisle towards the instrument – we could see the pipes, mounted high up on the left-hand wall near the altar, but couldn't see anybody actually playing the thing – the music seemed to fill my entire body until my very bones were throbbing with the vibrations of it.

We stood there for a while in the aisle, listening to it. Feeling it. There were two or three sustained chords, then suddenly the music came to an end, and it's funny but both Jaz and I started to clap. Not sarcastic, thank-Christ-that's-over type clapping; no, it was proper, appreciative applause, as if we were at a concert. What was weird about it was that we both started together, at exactly the same nanosecond, as if compelled by something outside of ourselves.

At the sound of our applauding, two startled heads popped up from behind one of the choir stalls directly underneath the organ pipes. I had a sudden buzzing in my ears that wasn't just from the music's reverberations.

"Oh, hi," said Lisa. She was pink, though whether from embarrassment at having been discovered *à deux* with Gabriel or pleasure at ditto, I wasn't sure. Her face – not big and round, like Mrs Cleaner had unflatteringly described it; it was maybe a tad on the round side, but I wouldn't have called it *big* – was lit up and glowing, as if from within.

Gabriel, on the other hand, looked totally laid-back and unmoved in any way, shape or form by Lisa's presence. Or ours, for that matter. "'Lo, girls," he said, lifting a laconic hand in greeting. "You liked my bit of Bach?"

"It . . . was . . . *amazing*," I pronounced. I looked at Jaz. Over her face was stealing the look that I was beginning to think of as The Gabriel Effect. Whoa, I thought. Looks like Patrice might have a bit of competition here.

I struggled to remain calm and composed as a foil to Jaz and Lisa's blatant hero-worship. Struggled, and failed. "Was it really you playing?"

"No, it was the Phantom of the Opera," Jaz scoffed, recovering from her reverie.

Lisa giggled. "You are funny, Jaz!"

"Well, it was hardly likely to have been you, was it?"

"Actually, I do play," Lisa squeaked indignantly. "Well, not the organ, but I do play the piano. And the flute." She came out from behind the choir stalls, looking flushed and slightly giddy. Presumably with joy at having been in such close proximity to Gabriel. "I'm actually really musical."

"So what are you doing here, then? Did you ask him to come over and accompany you on your flute, or something?" I didn't mean to sound sarcastic, but I'd felt oddly narked at the sight of her sat cosied up side-by-side with Gabriel on the organ bench.

"No!" Lisa tittered, and put a hand up to her mouth. "Course not! I haven't even got my flute with me.

When Gabriel said he was coming over to do some organ practice I said I'd come and turn his pages for him. Didn't I, Gabe?"

"I'll bet you did," Jaz said, under her breath, but more amused than bitchy. Through my head went the thought, *Gabe? How come she's got to call him Gabe already?*

Gabriel switched off the light that illuminated the organ console and, picking up the large volume of music that sat on the music stand and tucking it under his arm, said, "Right. I'll be off home then, seeing as your friends have turned up."

"But . . . but. . ." Lisa stammered, the happy giddy expression disappearing and being replaced by one of major disappointment that this was clearly the end of their shared musical experience. "How are we going to get out? Don't you have to lock up? Perhaps we should come with you," she added hopefully, but Gabriel shook his head.

"No, it's OK. Mrs Thingummy's come to do the hoovering, look. She'll lock up when she's finished."

Sure enough, at the back of the church we could see a woman pulling a vacuum cleaner along by its hose, looking for somewhere to plug it in.

"We could come with you anyway," I suggested. "Perhaps Bex is back now." It somehow felt desperately important to keep him with us for as long as possible.

(I know – pathetic. He was hardly going to invite us all on a triple date, after all.)

He shrugged good-naturedly. "Up to you. I think she's out for the day, though. I've got stuff to do, but you can stay here as long as you like. I'm sure Dad'd be thrilled if you took a look round. He's always keen on getting young people into his church. I'm told the stained glass in the chancel is particularly good."

He grinned at us again and was gone, loping elegantly down the aisle. It would have been impossible to follow him without scurrying along behind him decidedly inelegantly, and looking like an abject lovesick fool to boot.

"Aaaaaahh!" Lisa let out a long sigh, clasping her hands to her chest as if she was about to invite us all to say a prayer with her. "Isn't he the *most*. . ." She trailed off adoringly, and Jaz nodded in an appraising, matter-of-fact fashion.

"Pretty darn hot, I'll give you that. I can see what Mattie was going on about."

"So what are you two doing here, then?" Lisa asked us.

"Oh, we were just passing the church and we heard the organ," I said, flapping an airy hand. "We guessed it was probably Gabriel playing, and that you were turning his pages for him."

Lisa's eyes opened wide. "Really? Wow! How did you know that?"

"We're psychic. Didn't you know?"

"She's winding you up. Don't take any notice," Jaz told her, grinning at me.

Lisa was obviously more gullible than I'd realized. Perhaps I ought to explain properly.

"We went round to Bex's, but the cleaner woman told us another one of Bex's friends had called round a bit earlier. I thought it must be you." I left out the bit about big round faces. I somehow didn't think Lisa would want to know that. "And then when she said this mystery girl had come over to the church with Gabriel. . ." I said, trailing off meaningfully.

Lisa giggled. "Well, I couldn't let that chance go by, could I!"

"So what brought you all this way to see Bex?" I kept my tone light although, truth be told, I was ever so slightly peeved that Lisa not only had my idea first, i.e. calling on Bex as a way of maybe catching a glimpse of her brother, but had got in first with Gabriel as well. Even though he hadn't seemed to realize she'd been there with him for any other reason than to – well, to turn his pages, as she'd said. I sometimes wonder if lads are just dim when it comes to reading signs from girls.

"All this way?" Lisa laughed. "I live here. It only took me about ten minutes to walk round. I thought you knew I lived in Combe Bridge!"

I couldn't imagine why she thought that, given I'd barely known who she was until about two weeks ago.

"Wow, that's handy," Jaz put in drily. "You'll be able to pop round whenever you like, won't you?"

Lisa laughed again, gaily. "Lucky me, eh!"

"So why *did* you go round to Bex's today?" I persisted, and then realized I sounded as if I was interrogating her. "Not that it matters. I'm just, erm, you know, interested," I added hurriedly.

"Well, Bex told me she's doing English next year, and I thought it'd be useful for her to read *Emma* before the start of term, like the rest of us. So I brought it round for her."

"You brought *Emma* round? What, you mean my copy?"

Lisa looked puzzled. "Your copy?"

"Yes – the copy I lent you the other week because you'd left yours at Jaz's."

Now it was Jaz's turn for looking puzzled. She turned to Lisa. "You did? How come? Far as I remember, you've only been to my place once."

"Ah . . . yes. . ." The tips of Lisa's ears turned pink. "That was a mistake. I couldn't find mine and I thought I'd left it at yours when we were finishing off our coursework that time. But then I found it in my room. I've still got yours at home, Mattie. I can let you have it back now."

"Oh, OK." When Lisa had originally told me about the book, it sounded to me as if she'd spent loads of time round at Jaz's. I'd clearly just misunderstood. "No worries."

"Cool. I'll bring it round for you some time, yeah? I've got mine here, look." Lisa delved into the oversized straw bag she had slung over her shoulder, and produced the book. "I think I'll go and drop it round for Bex anyway. I can always leave it with the cleaner lady."

I was all set to go with her, but Jaz stopped me. "How about you 'n' me go and get an ice cream? Virgilio's in Combe Bridge does the *best* old-school Knickerbocker Glory ever."

"That sounds like a great idea. I might come and join you when I'm done." Beaming happily at us both, Lisa shoved the book back in her bag and trotted off down the aisle in the direction Gabriel had gone.

Chapter Six

Why is it that whenever I start getting excited about anything, along comes something to spoil it? Or in this instance, some*one*. Namely, Mommy Dearest.

Though, to be fair, it was my own fault: she overheard me on the phone to Jaz, discussing arrangements. I knew there was going to be trouble as soon as I put the phone down and went into the sitting room.

"A *party*?" she said, before I could utter a word, her eyebrows doing that disappearing-into-the-hair thing mums' eyebrows do so well. Or perhaps it's just my mother's facial hair that does contortions. "Remind me: when did I say you could have a party?"

Oops – busted. . .

"It's not really going to be a party," I lied. "More a little, erm, get-together."

"I distinctly heard you mention the word 'party'. I'm quite sure I never agreed to that."

"You kind of did." I went into wheedling mode. "Aw, go on, Mummykins. You did say I could have some friends round when you and Geoffy Baby are away for your anniversary weekend."

"Don't call him that." Mum frowned slightly. "I was thinking of one or two of your girlfriends. I didn't mean you could have a party. I've heard about these teenage parties when parents are away. Valerie Potter was telling me the other day about her granddaughter, who was invited to a friend's fifteenth-birthday party where a gang of yobs turned up and thrashed the place."

"Trashed."

"Sorry?"

"Trashed. You mean trashed, not thrashed." I sighed. "Like I'd let anything like that happen. Nice to be trusted."

"It's not a case of trust, darling. According to Mrs Potter, word of the party had got out at the girls' school and these boys just turned up. They drank all the alcohol in the house, and were smashing up furniture and all kinds of things. Her granddaughter was terrified."

I mentally put Andy at the top of the guest list. Not, as Jaz had suggested, as my potential love interest, but as chief bouncer. Having large male Upper Sixth friends could clearly come in handy in ways I'd never considered before.

"Chill, Mum." I gestured airily in her direction. "It's not going to happen."

"You're absolutely right it's not going to happen. There's not going to be a party. You can each have one friend over on Saturday for the evening – you, Molly and Rupert – and that's it. It's no good arguing, Mattie." She held up a hand to me like a policeman stopping the traffic. "There's an end to it."

And that, it appeared, was that. Leaving me opening and closing my mouth like a landed fish, and wondering where Hippy Dippy Laid-Back Mum had gone and how she'd been replaced by this firm, decisive Mum looky-likey, who strode purposefully from the room with a rustle of her silk peasant skirt.

She was replaced in about three seconds flat by Molly, who must have been standing outside the door, listening.

"Cheers, Mat." My sister pouted at me sulkily.

"What? What have I done?"

"Oh, nothing. Only gone and ruined my one chance for having a decent life, that's all. Nothing serious."

Sometimes, she acts so damn teenage-y she's like a walking cliché. Irritated, I clicked my tongue and folded my arms across my chest.

"So how did I do that, then? Go on – amaze me."

"I was going to have Chloë and Tasha and all that lot round when Mum and Geoffrey were away, and now I can't."

"And that's my fault because. . .?"

"Because now Mum says we can only have one friend each. Because you had to have your phone conversation about *parties* at ninety-thousand decibels, instead of being – what's the word?"

"Discweet," came a familiar voice from the doorway.

I turned. "Oh God," I groaned, "not you as well. I wasn't being *that* loud."

"You so were," Molly protested. "You were *screeching*. I could hear you upstairs. They could probably hear you down on the beach."

"I could hear you from outside," Rupert put in. "No wonder your mum overheard and put the kibosh on it."

I felt distinctly got at. "So what's it to you? Don't tell me – you were secretly planning to have a party, too. You little raver, you."

Rupert's face remained totally impassive. "Well, actually, I was," he said.

Molly and I both stared at him.

"No way! Who on earth were you going to invite?" I demanded. The idea of Rupert throwing a party in the parental absence was so unlikely, it was almost funny.

"No need to look so supwised. I do have fwends, you know," he replied, slightly huffily.

Molly started to grin. "Wow, Rupes. Respect!"

She high-fived him, and his face broke into a smile. I don't think I had ever seen him properly smile before.

Which is quite sad, when you come to think of it. I mean, he'd been part of our lives for, what, eighteen months or so, and up till that point I'd never seen him crack his face with anything other than a smug, self-satisfied upturning of the mouth, a parody of a smile that stopped way short of his eyes. It was such an unfamiliar expression to see on his face, I could feel myself staring at him.

"Well, maybe not a party exactly. Not as such," he was saying. "But I'd asked Michael to come over, and Cwispin and Oliver fwom school. They were going to bwing sleeping bags, and we were going to stay up all night and play internet Dungeons and Dwagons."

It was the longest speech I'd heard him make, and the most animated. A smile, a proper conversation: could it be that my stepbrother was turning from pondlife into, well, practically a human being? (Despite the extreme dweebiness of what he and his little friends had in mind to fill their time.)

Molly began to giggle. "So all three of us had planned to have loads of mates round while they were away! Maybe it's just as well Mum found out. We'd never have all fitted in!"

She had a point. There is a word to describe our house now there's five of us living in it, and that word is snug. I pulled a rueful face. "Sorry, guys. Looks like I've messed it up for everyone."

"Doesn't matter." Rupert pursed his lips and did a funny little side-to-side movement with his head, looking like a bonsai version of his father. Geoffrey does exactly the same thing as a kind of No Worries response. "Alice said one fwend each," he went on, "so Michael can still come, and we can still play internet games. And Molly can still have Chloë, and you can still have Jaz. Can't you?"

I wondered why he was being so reasonable. If I were him I'd have been well ticked-off at me for scuppering his arrangements. Then I remembered – he'd had a major crush on Jaz for months. Perhaps he fancied his chances with her if he were alone in the house with her. Well, alone-ish, not counting me, Moll, Chloë and Michael. (So not alone at all, then.)

"I can, yeah," I agreed. "But don't hold your breath. The only scoring you're likely to be doing is at your Dungeons and Dwagons. Sorry, I mean Dragons."

It was mean, I know. Only a couple of months ago he'd have turned a furious bright red at the dig, pressed his lips together in a thin line, and stomped off. But to his credit, he did none of those things. Instead, he grinned sheepishly at me.

"I know. But a guy can dweam, can't he?"

Huh. Fat lot of good dreaming did him. Not that I'm blaming Rupert's daydreams of him and Jaz, wandering hand in slo-mo hand through a field of poppies (or whatever it was he was imagining) for what happened. That would be plain stupid. But it was odd how all my plans of what larks I was going to have in the absence of Mum and Geoffrey went from full-on party to well, nothing, within a matter of minutes.

Don't you just love it when your mates make it plain they've got a better offer? No, me neither.

"What, you mean no party? Not at all?" Jaz said, when I finally got through to her after Mum finished on the phone. God knows who she'd been talking to, but she'd been hogging it for about an hour.

"Not even a teensy-weensy one." I tried to make my voice sound upbeat. "But it's cool. You can still come and stay over, and we can have pizza and make popcorn and all that. And I'll get Geoffy Baby to take me to town on Friday, and I'll hire a whole pile of vids from Blockbuster's. Is there anything you fancy seeing?"

I knew it would be a pretty poor substitute for an actual party. Jaz – whose parents are loaded – has her own DVD player in her room, along with a whole stack of state-of-the-art electronic toys. It looks like a branch of Currys. Not only that, but she buys all the latest DVDs as soon as they come out. Videos are old hat to her. There'd be nothing I could offer her to watch that she hadn't already seen a hundred times before.

But I wasn't expecting her response. There was a silence, the sort that's described in books as a pregnant pause, and my heart sank.

"Ma-at," she began kindly. My heart sank even further. "I've really gone and messed up for Saturday. Would you be dead annoyed with me if I didn't come?"

How could I answer that? I listened, umming and erring in all the right places as she explained that it was her dad's work summer barbecue on Saturday night, and her parents really wanted her to go along as her dad's boss had this totally fit son they wanted to fix her up with. I think that's how it went. I was just wondering where Patrice (*L'Homme Extraordinaire*) fitted into the equation when I realized I was listening to silence. Obviously my turn to speak.

"Umm," I said. "Is this going to be an arranged marriage, kind of thing?"

How Jaz laughed. "Don't be a doughnut! Of course it isn't! But Pa had already told me and Surjit about the barbecue when we were in France, before you even mentioned your party, and it *is* his boss, so. . ." I imagined her doing one of her elaborate shrugs. *So go figure. Daddy wanting to get in with the boss vs Mattie's stupid little overnighter? No-brainer.*

She was talking again. "You've gone all quiet. You *are* annoyed with me, aren't you?" She does this sometimes: turns things around so it's my annoyance, my decision, my fault. If she'd asked me if I was upset, or disappointed, it would have been better, but annoyed? How could I answer and not sound childish?

"Not exactly annoyed," I started carefully.

"You are. I can tell. Listen, Mat, just say if you really want me to come over, and I will. It's just – well – if it was a proper party at yours it would be different, but we can do a sleepover any time, can't we? And it is important to Pa that Surjit and me are there – it's a real family thing. And apparently, Mr Farrington-Haugh opens the champagne at six, when everyone arrives, and it's still going strong at midnight! You do understand, don't you? Hmmm?"

And so I found myself agreeing with her that yes, I understood, and yes, of course we could postpone our sleepover to a more mutually convenient time (i.e., when she had a window in her busy social calendar), and as I put the phone down I felt so let down I almost burst into tears. I know – pathetic.

I was just debating ringing Bex and asking her instead – even though we barely knew each other well enough for me to invite her to what would blatantly be an evening of being quizzed about her brother – when the phone rang virtually under my nose, making me jump.

"Hiya, Mattie," said the bright and breezy voice on the other end.

An evening of quizzing Bex about her brother. . .

A little light bulb went on in my brain. *Ping. . .*

"Hi, Lisa," I said thoughtfully. "Listen, are you doing anything on Saturday night?"

REASONS FOR ADORING GABRIEL:
1) *His face!!*
2) *His eyes!!*
3) *His lips (when smiling or otherwise)!!*
4) *His hair!!*
5) *His smooth, suntanned, muscly six-pack. . .*
6) *. . .in fact, his smooth, suntanned, muscly bod in general!!*
7) *His *cough* bum!!*
8) *His sense of humour!!*
9) *His name!!*
10) *He can drive. And gives his sister lifts, so is kind.*
11) *He likes animals, so is kind and sensitive.*
12) *He speaks French. Fluently, according to Bex. So is clever, kind and sensitive :o)*
13) *He skis. And snowboards. So is sporty, clever, kind and sensitive :o) :o)*
14) *Oh bugger it. Just HIM!!! HE ROCKS!!!!!*

Lisa put my diary down and looked up at me, her eyes shining. "Oh my *God*! That could have been written by me! I never realized you felt the same as me about him. He is just so incredible, isn't he?"

And she was off.

Now, I wouldn't normally show my diary to anybody – even Jaz had only ever read edited highlights – but as I was being deprived of a) my party, and b) Jaz's company, the next best thing was the prospect of a nice girly self-indulgent evening in, salivating over my Hottie of the Moment with someone who shared a similar point of view.

The evening began well when Lisa arrived carrying a four-pack of Bacardi Breezers and two tubs of Pringles. First hairslides, now drinks and snacks . . . I made a mental note to invite her round more often.

As we popped the first Pringles, the sound of Kylie being played at ninety-thousand decibels drifted (if drifted is the right word) from upstairs, where Molly was barricaded in our room with Chloë.

"What is it you're doing next year, then?" Lisa asked me

"Huh?"

"What subjects. In the sixth form. Apart from English Lit, of course; I know you're doing that! Hey, where d'you keep your bottle opener?"

I got up and opened the dresser drawer. "Here you go." I handed it to her. "I haven't totally made up my mind on subjects yet. Depends on my results, really."

Lisa put her hands up to her face and let out a little

squeal. "Oh my God! The results! They're out next week, I'd totally forgotten!"

I wished I had. They'd been preying on my mind from the moment I'd put the lid back on my pen after the final exam. "Hang on a minute." I went to the bottom of the stairs and shouted. "Oi, Molly! Turn it down a bit, will you!"

No response. If anything, the music just got louder.

I went upstairs and bashed on the door, and when there was still no answer I pushed it open and went in. Chloë was sitting at the desk (which doubles as a dressing table), puckering up, while Molly was applying bright red lipgloss to her mouth. *My* bright red lipgloss, unless I was very much mistaken. I took a surprised step backwards, and noticed a whole load of familiar-looking clothes spread across my bed. Yup, you've guessed it. They looked familiar because they were mine.

They didn't hear me come in because of the volume of the music – Kylie was still "Spinning Around" at a volume that was actually making the windows rattle in their frames – but Chloë must have spotted me in the mirror, because she let out a little gasp. Molly wheeled round, startled, then leapt to the CD player and fiddled with the volume control.

"Oh, hi, Mat." Fake cheesy grin, apologetic body language. "I didn't think you'd mind if we just. . ." She trailed off.

The joys of sharing a room with your little sister. Under normal circumstances I'd have gone mental with her, but the prospect of spending a deliciously girly evening with Lisa discussing the ins and outs (as it were) of the Gorgeous Gabriel, plus the fact I wanted to appear as Tolerant Older Sister rather than Clone of Mother, made me unusually mellow. Or perhaps it was the tumbler of vodka and Red Bull I'd downed before Lisa had arrived. Whatever – I just wanted to get downstairs and on with the evening's main agenda, and couldn't be bothered to get arsey with her.

I raised a casually forbearing hand and said, "That's fine. Just clear up after yourselves, yeah?"

When I got back downstairs, Lisa was in the hall talking animatedly on the telephone. She looked up at me and smiled, still talking.

"Yeah, OK babe, that's fine. Here she is." She handed the receiver to me and smiled again. "It rang while you were upstairs, and I thought I'd better answer it in case it was an emergency. Hope that's OK?"

"Yeah, sure." I took the receiver from her hand. "Hello?"

"Mattie?" It was Jaz.

"Hiya!" I was disproportionately delighted to hear her voice. "How's the barbecue going?"

"Utter crap," she growled. "The boss is a lech and the

boss's son is a total minger. I wish I'd come round to yours now. Who's that who answered your phone?"

"It's Lisa."

"Who?"

"Lisa. Lisa! You know – Lisa Gray?"

"Oh, right." There was a small pause. "Since when did you get so chummy with Lisa Gray?"

"Well, you couldn't come, so. . ." I shrugged, then realized she couldn't see me. "I had to have *someone* to keep me company while the olds are away. Molly's upstairs with her little friend raiding the contents of my wardrobe and make-up bag, and Rupert's playing nerdy internet games with your next-door neighbour."

Jaz made a short noise that sounded more like a bark than a laugh. "Sounds a whole lot better than being groped behind the privet by an Austin Powers looky-likey."

"You're kidding! Is that the father or the son?"

"Both. The Austin Powers thing, at any rate. The groping was just the son."

"Aww. I wish you could have come round here instead."

"So do I. But hey. . ." She gave a gusty sigh. "Isn't it about time you got a moby? So we can chat in private, not on some landline that the whole of your family can overhear? If not the whole of Brandy Bay."

I wish. . . "I'm working on it, OK?" *Just as soon as my mother and stepfather enter this millennium.*

So in due course we said our goodbyes and hung up, and when I went back into the kitchen Lisa handed me an opened bottle with one hand and a bowl of Pringles with the other.

"Is that your diary?" she said, indicating with her head the dresser where I'd left it earlier, kind of accidentally-on-purpose, as a prop should conversation flag.

"Not a diary as such. More a journal." I opened it up at the Gabriel page, and that was us for the rest of the evening. We had a blast.

Chapter Seven

Combe Bridge is set at the end of a steep-sided valley, where the river hastens to its end before meandering out to the sea, and St Mark's (the school, that is) is situated high above the village. One of the first things I remember when we moved down here was driving through Combe Bridge with Mum and Moll on our way to Brandy Bay, our new home and new life, and seeing this large, imposing-looking building perched up behind the streets and the harbour, looming over everything. It was Molly, as I recall, squashed up on the back seat among the bedding and towels swathed in black bin liners, who pointed to it as we drove past and asked what it was.

"It's a school," Mum said distractedly, peering at the road signs at the set of crossroads we'd just stopped at. "It's where Mattie will be going next year."

Sitting in relative comfort next to Mum – comfort, that is, apart from the budgie in the ornate white wrought-iron cage balanced distinctly uncomfortably on my knee – my heart sank to my boots. (Or sensible Clarks lace-ups, which I was more likely to have been wearing, being ten at the time.) There was something about the building that looked forbidding, dour and brooding, although that might have had more to do with the rain that was beating rhythmically against the windscreen, driven hard by a spiteful swirling November wind that ripped the remaining few leaves from the trees and whipped the waves in the just-visible harbour to a froth of churning foam. Or perhaps it was just an all-too-visible reminder of the changes that had been imposed upon my little life in such a short space of time, changes which, although welcome (I wouldn't have wished my old life, with a drunken, abusive father – when he was there – on anybody), were nonetheless pretty much total. Everything familiar had been swept away, and was being replaced by new, unfamiliar things: new location, new home, new friends, new school. And here, sat on the hillside above and scowling down on us, or so it seemed to me, was another new school to add to the equation.

I was only in Year Six, so my education was the last thing I'd considered when Mum had first told us we were moving from Manchester to Devon, but I considered it then, all right. The penny dropped with a deafening clang that I'd only be in my new class for a couple of terms, and then it would be time to go off to Big School. And not just any old Big School, but this one. I didn't like the thought one little bit.

I liked it scarcely more when the following September came round and off I went, although I'd made new friends by then, of course, and most of us went there together. My worries then were more concerned with How Will I Find My Way Round Such a Big Place, and Will the New Teachers be as Nice as Mrs Browning Was, and Will the Older Kids Stick Us Newbies' Heads Down the Bogs and Flush Them (yup, that old chestnut), all of which I've since gathered are pretty common anxieties at that particular rite of passage.

Arriving at school now, my first day of becoming that most elevated of beings (yeah, right!), A Sixth Former, I suddenly remembered all my heebie-jeebies of more than six years previously and wondered what on earth I'd been so scared of. It's not a bad school, as schools go. In fact, I'd even go so far as to say it's a pretty damn fine school. And on a day like today, with the sun shining and the blue of the sky reflected in the sea far below, you could even feel a certain – y'know – gladness, pride even, at being a student there. It commands a pretty spectacular position, too. Not that the view seemed to be impressing the little knots of tiny people loitering apprehensively at the gates, or scurrying nervously across the tarmac. Year Sevens, clearly, with their too-big, too-smart, just-too-damn-*new* uniforms. Newbies. Me, six years ago. Surely I was never that small?

Feeling suddenly sorry for them (or possibly sorry for my eleven-year-old self back then), I approached a little group of them on my way in through the double front doors, an entrance only permissible for staff and sixth-formers.

"Don't worry," I said to them, with a kindly and reassuring smile. "It's quite nice here, really. You'll be fine."

"Who was that?" I heard one of them hiss behind my departing back.

"Teacher," another replied with confidence.

Is it sad to get a kick out of being mistaken for a teacher? OK then, guilty as charged. I'm officially sad. I sashayed into the front hall with a new spring in my step, feeling über-cool, until a stern male voice called out behind me and stopped me in my tracks.

"You, girl – Matilda Fry! What are you doing coming through this entrance?"

I wheeled round, startled, but the sheepish explanation about now being in the sixth form died on my lips as soon as I saw who my interrogator was.

"Andy!" I exclaimed. "You bugger!"

He chortled. "Last year's Upper Sixth hung round in

here last year and did it to all us lot. Got us every time. You're my first victim."

"Don't worry, I won't hold it against you." I was ridiculously pleased to see him. I threw my arms round him in a big enthusiastic hug. "Aw, it's really good to see you!"

He hugged me back, obediently if not quite as wholeheartedly, and when we drew apart he stood there looking slightly embarrassed, shuffling from foot to foot. "I thought you said you weren't going to hold it against me."

"Ha ha. You know what I meant. So how's things? How were your AS levels?"

"Yeah, good. How about you? Got the results you wanted?"

It's funny with exams, isn't it? You wait for ages for the wretched things to happen, then even longer for the results, and then when they've finally arrived and you've gone into school to pick them up you realize it's only half the story, because your friends have had their results, too. Standing in the main hall where they were being handed out, and grasping my unexpectedly good clutch of A-stars and As (plus a couple of Bs and a C just to make sure I didn't get too big-headed), I suddenly noticed that not everybody was looking as happy as me. Dilemma: how do you swap grades with your mates when they're obviously not as pleased with theirs as you are with yours? When somebody comes up to you with that brave Oh Shit look on their face and asks how you did, what do you say? *Bloody fantastic! Over the moon!* (i.e., the truth), or the less honest but distinctly more diplomatic *Oh, not too bad, thanks*? Do you politely ask them in return how they did, or just take the look on their face as the answer? And if I found it was hard to cope with the disappointment of some of my mates in the light of my own good results, I could only imagine how tough it would be had the boot been on the other foot, and I'd messed up. Tell you what – this whole exam thing is fraught with social complications they never tell you about when they send out the arrangements for Results Day.

I decided modest quipping was the way to go with Andy. "Pretty much." I shrugged. "They've let me back in, at any rate."

"I'll tell you who they didn't let back in," he remarked as we strolled over to the sixth-form block together. "Sam."

"Sam? God! Why not?"

"Well, the official story is his parents decided this isn't the right place for him, they're furious with school for letting him down, yadda yadda yadda."

"And the unofficial one?"

"He got three Es. Deserved it too, the clown. He didn't do a stroke of work all year. Too busy with the laydeez." He glanced at me and pulled a face. "Oops. Sorry, Mat. Sore point."

"No, no," I protested, although Andy's comment had in fact given me a pang – one of pure relief at the news that Sam wouldn't be returning. "It's fine. Water under the bridge. All done and dusted."

We'd got to the top of the stairs to the sixth-form block, and Andy held the door open for me with an ironic bow. "Ta daa. Welcome to my world, Ms Fry."

The sixth-form block at St Mark's is coolness squared. As well as a big communal area with sofas, beanbags etc., and study booths behind a partition at one end, there's a small kitchen/dining area down some steps at the other end. It's fully equipped with kettle, microwave, fridge-freezer, cooker, hob, sink, cupboards for storage – in fact, everything needed for preparing our own lunch, should we want to opt out of the school dinners that were brought up for us, as well as the various snack-stops throughout the day. As I stood at the top of the steps, wishing I'd had the foresight to bring some coffee and stuff along with my sandwiches, Lisa emerged from the kitchen clutching a steaming mug. She beamed when she saw me.

"Hiya, Mattie! Fancy a cuppa? The kettle's just boiled."

"Is that coffee? You're a mind-reader! I was just thinking I should have brought some in."

Lisa pulled a rueful face. "Nooo, it's hot water and lemon. I think I saw a jar in the cupboard, though."

"Hot water and lemon? What, are you on a health kick or something?" I grinned.

"I'm trying to lose some weight. I've put on so much over the holidays – look." She put the mug down on a table and pulled at about a centimetre of spare flesh above the waistband of her cropped trousers. "It's just as well we can wear our own clothes for sixth form. I'd never have got into my uniform."

"God, tell me about it! The problem with having a decent summer for once is that it's just way too easy to eat too many ice creams to cool down."

"Don't know what you're on about." Andy came down the stairs two at a time, bearing a bulging Tesco's carrier bag. "You both look fine to me. I don't know why you girlies are always going on about how much you weigh. Who wants to go out with a stick insect?"

"Another stick insect?" I suggested, with a lads-eh-what-do-they-know wink at Lisa.

"Precisely. No lad I know has any objections to a few curves. Me, I much prefer a lass with a bit of meat on her."

"Aah, Andy, you silver-tongued smoothie, you," I cooed at him. "You certainly know how to woo the ladies. So go on, then. What's in your bag?"

"Coffee, milk, sugar, custard creams." He produced them from the bag in the manner of a contestant on *Ready Steady Cook*. "And. . ." He peeped inside and then looked mischievously at us over the top. "Ze secret ingredient – ze chocolate HobNobs!"

He whipped them out with a flourish, and even though it wasn't yet nine o'clock in the morning, my mouth watered.

"Ooh, yum. Can I have one?"

"Only if you give me a big kiss and tell me how much you love me. . . Joking!" he said hastily as I bore down on him, puckering up. "Want a HobNob, Lisa?"

"No, no, you're all right." She wrapped both her hands protectively round her mug. "Lemon and hot water's really nice, once you get used to it."

I went up the stairs to the main area, where I could see Jaz talking animatedly with someone. Someone short and petite with spiked blonde hair, and ripped black tights worn under the world's teensiest tartan skirt.

"Bex!" I gave her a hug. It was like embracing one of those Year Sevens. "Welcome to the madhouse! I see you've met Jaz already."

"I can't believe Bex and I never got round to meeting up in the holidays!" Jaz exclaimed. "We've got so much in common, it's ludicrous. We got identical GCSE results, we're doing the same subjects, and guess what? We were born in the same hospital!"

I turned to Bex. "I didn't know you were born in Devon."

"I wasn't. I was born in London."

"Same as me!" I hadn't seen Jaz as animated as this for ages. "My parents were living in London for a bit while my dad was doing his junior registrar year."

Jaz has been my best mate the entire time I've been living in Brandy Bay, and I never knew that about her. An odd prickly sensation shot through me.

"*And* you've both got hot brothers," Lisa put in coquettishly from behind me. Jaz and Bex exchanged meaningful glances. Bex had already made it plain to Lisa and me how fed up she got when girls just wanted to talk about her brother, so Lisa was on a hiding to nothing. She was hardly going to ingratiate herself with Bex with that kind of comment.

"So how's your timetable shaping up?" I asked Jaz hastily, changing the subject.

"Actually, I've made a couple of last-minute swaps. I'm doing English, French, German and history now," Jaz told me.

"Aww." I felt really disappointed. "That means we'll only be in English together. I thought you were going to do geography?"

"They let me switch." Jaz shrugged. "I always fancied

doing history, but I didn't think I'd get such a good grade. Hey, Mat, I'm loving your hairclip. Where d'you get it?"

I couldn't remember which one I'd put on that morning, and put my hand up to the back of my head to remind myself. It was Lisa's Aztec one.

"I gave it to her," Lisa said, before I could reply. "It's nice, isn't it? It really suits your colouring. You've got such fab hair."

She touched my head, prattling about natural highlights or some such, and Jaz and Bex started chatting again before wandering off together, leaving me with the unpleasant but distinct impression that I cared a whole lot more about the prospect of hardly seeing Jaz in lessons than Jaz did herself.

Predictably, Bex attracted loads of attention. Less predictably, she seemed to be a big hit with the boys. I thought I knew the lads at St Mark's pretty well, or certainly the ones in my year, and I never suspected they'd be drawn to – well, I don't mean this in a bitchy way, but to a grunge/punk/rock-chick gal with the dress sense of a charity shop regular. Yet here they all were, fawning over Bex as if she were some exotic zoo creature. It was quite funny, really. Especially as it was plain that she wasn't interested in any of them.

"Look at them all," I remarked to Jaz at lunch time.

We were sitting together at one of the tables in the sixth-form kitchen bit, eating our sandwiches. (At least, I was eating my sandwiches. Jaz was eating her quiche, pitta bread with hummus, barbecued chicken leg, mini party-eggs, family-sized plastic container filled with salad, and whatever the hell else she'd brought for lunch. I don't know where she puts it all, and the really irritating thing is, she is built not like Vanessa Feltz, but Kate Moss. The ratbag.)

"Hmm?" Jaz said distractedly, fiddling with her phone whilst simultaneously stuffing a party-egg into her mouth. "Look at who?"

"Whom. Look at *whom*." I sometimes wish I could stop this compulsion I have for correcting other people's grammar, but it's like a knee-jerk reaction. Luckily for me, nobody takes any notice any more.

Jaz stopped fiddling and looked at me. "What? What are you on about?"

"Look at all the hopefuls round Bex. Like dogs round a bitch on heat. It's quite sad really."

"It's not that surprising, though, is it? She's interesting."

"Only because she's new. Look at Brad Smythe! If he grins at her any more his face is going to split in half."

Jaz gave me a funny look. "It's not only because she's new. You don't really think that, do you? I thought you liked her. I think she's totally cool."

"Oh, so do I," I agreed. "I like her loads. I was just saying that it's quite funny to watch all the lads posing round her."

"Right." She went back to her phone again, and I sensed I'd lost her. A little spurt of annoyance ran through me.

"What're you doing?"

"Hmm? Oh, it's a text from Patrice."

I might have guessed. "So is he missing you madly?"

She grinned. "He is, actually. Bless. So hey –" She put the phone down at last, and leant a bit closer towards me in a conspiratorial manner. "How come Lisa's been giving you presents?"

I put an instinctive hand up to the back of my head, and the Aztec hairclip. "She hasn't. Well, not exactly presents. It was just a thank-you for doing her a favour, kind of thing."

"Right." There was something in her tone that made me carry on.

"Why d'you ask?"

"Oh, nothing." She lifted a dismissive shoulder. "It's just. . ."

"Just. . .?"

"Well, I didn't think you even knew her. But then I come back from France to find you're bosom buddies all of a sudden – she's giving you presents, answering your phone of a Saturday night. . ."

"We're not bosom buddies!" I laughed. The very idea was ridiculous. In fact, if I didn't know Jaz better I'd have said she sounded jealous. But then, that was ridiculous, too.

"If you say so. But . . . she can be very over-emotional, haven't you found? A bit highly strung?"

"Really? Can't say I've noticed." I felt oddly defensive, although I wasn't sure why. "I thought you said you didn't know her that well? You didn't even know which Lisa I meant when I mentioned her first."

"I don't know her that well. But when we were doing that coursework together last year, she . . . well, she was a bit strange. Or I thought she could *get* strange, if I encouraged her."

"I don't understand." I peeled the top off my yoghurt, carefully, and licked the lid. I didn't want to admit it, but I knew exactly what she meant.

"It's like . . . she got really worked up about the slightest thing, Mat. Not with me, I don't mean. She was always fine with me. In fact, that was the problem. It was like she suddenly considered me to be her new best friend. We were supposed to be doing work together, but we hardly did anything. We'd sit in the library and she'd spend hours telling me about her latest boyfriend troubles, or whatever."

"So you fell out? Is that what you're saying?"

"No, nothing like that. But she was so intense, and it

got to the point where I kind of felt. . ." Jaz trailed off abruptly and looked up, smiling. "Oh, hi, Lisa."

Lisa, holding a plate with an apple on it, was beaming down on us. "Can I join you?"

"Sure," I said, but Jaz pushed her chair back with a scrape.

"God, is that the time? I've got to go and see Miss Matthews about French convo classes. Catch up with you later, yeah?"

"Jaz, don't forget your lunch box!" Lisa called, brandishing it with a flourish, but it was too late. Jaz had gone. "Boy, was she in a hurry!" Lisa exclaimed, with a giggle. "The silly – she's left half her lunch, look!"

Chapter Eight

A week or so into the new term, a notice appeared on the pinboard in the sixth-form block. ST MARK'S PLAYERS, it proclaimed in a large shouty font on bright yellow paper – the sort of fluorescent Post-it notes yellow that's not easily overlooked. Definitely a notice to be noticed, then.

Further inspection revealed it not to be St Mark's as in the school, but as in the church.

"Did you put that up there?" I asked Bex.

"What she means is, did you get permission from Mr Harbrace?" Lisa said.

I hadn't meant that, but Bex pulled a face. "It's only a poxy *notice*. Why do I need to get permission from Mr Fartface?"

Lisa giggled, putting her hand up to her mouth. "Well, he *is* the head of sixth form. He gets dead upset if people put stuff up on the board without asking."

"How d'you know what he gets upset about? You've only been in the sixth form five minutes, like the rest of us." Jaz stepped forward to take a closer look, and Lisa pouted slightly.

"I thought it was common knowledge that Mr Harbrace gets all possessive about the noticeboard. It's, like, legendary."

Next to me, I sensed Jaz limbering up for a spot of oh-no-it-isn't. She's got a bit of a thing about people claiming to be in the know about stuff that, in her opinion, they can have no experience of.

"Never mind Mr Harbrace and his noticeboard, what's this all about?" I asked Bex. "I've never heard of St Mark's Players. Is it something your dad's starting?"

She explained that the group, which met in the church hall, had apparently been going for years. "It's an am-dram society. Nothing to do with my dad," she said. "It's run by one of the parishioners. Mrs Pym. She came round last night, said she's desperately trying to get some younger members to join. She's been trying to establish links with schools for ages but with no luck, so I said I'd put some notices up round school. I didn't think I'd have to ask permission."

"I'm sure it'll be fine," I told her. "I mean, it's kind of educational, isn't it? Can't say it's my cup of tea, though."

"Hey, look, they're doing *Grease* next term. I think it sounds quite fun," Lisa said, looking thoughtful.

Jaz pulled a face. "Sounds about as much fun as self-amputation to me. No offence, Bex."

"None taken. It's nothing to do with me, like I said. I'm just being the dutiful vicar's daughter."

"What about you, Mattie? Wouldn't you be interested in going along? Rehearsals start this week – look."

I couldn't understand why Lisa was persisting in the face of such conspicuous lack of enthusiasm from us. "Well, I would do, except I can't act, I can't dance and I can't sing. They're not exactly going to welcome me with open arms, trust me."

"Don't be so hard on yourself! *Everyone* can sing, if they try."

Jaz snorted. "You obviously haven't heard Mattie try. She gives the phrase 'tone deaf' a whole new meaning."

Well, what could I say? She was absolutely right. When I was about eight I'd been desperate to be in my old school choir because they wore ribbons on the ends of their pigtails instead of elastic bands (or the girls did, at any rate), and got to miss lessons and go on a coach to sing at festivals and suchlike. I only got to sing in it the once; as soon as the practice started, a horrified look began to slide over the face of Mrs McLeish, the teacher who conducted it. *Just open and close your mouth in time with the music, dear*, she suggested to me. *No need to actually make any noise.* And that was the end of my glittering career in the school choir.

Lisa started to protest, saying that being properly tone deaf was a really rare thing and I'd probably just had a bad experience of singing when I was little (so true: eat your heart out, Mrs McLeish), when I suddenly spotted it. There, lurking at the bottom of the notice in teensy-weensy little letters were the words *Director/Producer: L. Pym*, and underneath them, in even teensier weensier letters, *Musical Director: I. Burnside, Accompanist: G. Foxcroft.*

I turned to Bex, but she'd clearly got bored with the whole topic and had wandered off to make herself a drink. I could see her down in the kitchen, surrounded by lads as usual.

"Do you know," I said to Lisa instead, "I think you may be right about the singing. Perhaps it's time to have another crack at it."

We agreed to meet outside the church hall just before the rehearsal that Wednesday. But I started to get cold feet before I'd even set one of them inside the place. What if (and yeah, OK, I know it was unlikely) there was another piano-playing G. Foxcroft kicking around the place? Wouldn't Bex have mentioned it if her brother was involved? And what if they expected me to – omigod the thought was so terrible I nearly turned tail and ran there and then – to *audition*?

But I didn't have a chance to run, because as I was

dithering around outside, battling with all these thoughts and waiting for Lisa, a large woman with maroon hair, dressed in the kind of long, flowing, hippyish garments my mum would have fallen on with cries of joy, came bounding up to me.

"Hello, hello," she boomed. "Have you come for *Grease*? Jolly good, splendid." And she kind of gathered me up and swept me in before I could so much as utter a squeak of protest.

Inside the hall, small knots of people were standing around in a desultory fashion, and I began to see why this L. Pym (for it was clearly she) had been so desperate to recruit some younger members. The average age of the ones here seemed to hover around sixty. Into my head popped a vision of *Grease* performed by a superannuated cast – a creakily rheumatic Danny, Sandy as a blue-rinsed pensioner – and I had a sudden urge to giggle.

Several of them greeted us as we came in, L. Pym sailing majestically along in the manner of a grand ocean-going liner scything through the waves, me scuttling along in her wake like a small, insignificant tug. Which is exactly how I felt. Where the hell was Lisa?

"Hello, Lynda! Lovely to see you again – we're so looking forward to *Grease*, aren't we, Percy?"

This last was from a tiny, smiley woman with a face

so brown and wrinkled she looked like a walnut. She turned to me encouragingly.

"And do I spy a new member? How lovely! Welcome, dear. You'll find us all very friendly."

I gulped nervously. She certainly seemed very friendly, but I still had the spectre of a possible audition looming before me.

"Will I have to – erm – sing?" I managed to stutter. "By myself? Like – I mean – an audition?"

The walnut-woman smiled again, and gave the little old man standing next to her a nudge. "Tell her about your audition, Percy."

My heart sank to my boots, but the man gave a broad grin and dug her in the ribs with his elbow. "Oh, you! Don't take any notice of Mavis, my duck. Nobody has to audition just to join. Reckon there wouldn't be many of us here if we did!"

Mavis-the-walnut-woman clicked her tongue affectionately. "Now you're making her think we're no good. What Perce means is, there's something for everybody here. If the acting thing isn't for you, there's always lots to be done backstage. That's what we do."

"Hiya." It was Lisa, tapping me on the shoulder and making me jump. I spun round.

"Blimey! Where did you spring from? You nearly gave me a heart attack!"

Mavis and Percy laughed heartily, as if the sight of

me dropping down dead from shock on the floor in front of them would have been just another of my funny ways.

"Oh, sorry," said Lisa. She looked flustered. "Sorry I'm a bit late. Did I miss anything?"

She looked over at the piano and empty piano stool in the corner of the hall, and I knew instantly what – or rather who – she meant.

"Nope. He's not here yet," I told her.

Lisa's face was a picture of innocent bewilderment. Obviously well practised at this acting lark, then. "Who isn't?"

"Oh, *dur*. The accompanist? A certain G. Foxcroft?"

She went pink, and grinned sheepishly. "Did you see his name on the notice too, then?"

"No, I'm just psychic." I grinned back. "Course I did. Isn't that why we're both here?"

The doors opened just then and a group of five or six girls came in, shoving each other and giggling. I recognized a couple of them as being in the same year as Moll at school. I gave Lisa a nudge.

"Looks as if Bex's notices round school did the trick. Unless I'm mistaken, that lot are in Year Nine."

Spotting them, Lynda Pym went over to where they stood, exclaiming delightedly at top volume. As well she might. Their presence, plus mine and Lisa's, had reduced the average age in the hall by about half. I did wonder when things were going to start, though. I'd already been there for nearly twenty minutes, and there was no sign of anything remotely *Grease*-like happening.

But just when I was beginning to think I'd been dragged there under false pretences, the double swing doors flew open and in came the vision of loveliness that was Gabriel. I say came, but he tripped as he opened the doors and actually half-fell, half-staggered into the hall, dropping most of the wad of sheet music he was carrying. Talk about making an entrance. The gaggle of Year Nines turned as one, staring at him open-mouthed as if unable to believe they shared a planet, let alone a church hall, with someone this gorgeous (a feeling, I might say, not unfamiliar to me).

"Bugger," he said, as bits of sheet music fluttered to the floor and slid across the polished wood. He knelt on one knee and began collect it all up. "Sorry, folks."

Some impulse propelled me forward, and I found myself on my hands and knees beside him.

"Here, let me. . ."

"Thanks." Our eyes met, briefly, and my heart stood still. Nobody had had this effect on me for ages, not since Sam. "What a div, eh. Born clumsy, that's me."

He started to whistle nonchalantly, and I couldn't help admiring his coolness. If it had been me dropping my music everywhere – and I'm sure, given the same circumstances, I could have been relied on to do just that – I'd have been mortified. But he hadn't even gone red.

He picked up the final piece and we stood up together, almost crashing heads in the process.

"Sorry!" We both laughed, and as he looked at me again he did a double take. "I thought I recognized you," he said. "You're my sister's mate, erm. . ."

"Mattie," I supplied, helpfully.

"Of course. Mattie. How could I forget?" He smiled at me, slowly, lazily, and my stomach did a backflip. He wasn't . . . surely he couldn't be *flirting* with me?

"It's me, too." Lisa was suddenly there beside me. She bobbed her head around, grinning slightly manically at him. "Remember me?"

"Sure. Erm, Lucy, right?"

But she didn't have time to correct him because just at that moment Lynda Pym clapped her hands together.

"Can we have a bit of hush, please, ladies and gents? I think most of us have already had the pleasure of making his acquaintance, but for those of you who haven't, may I just introduce our vicar's son, Gabriel Foxcroft? He's very kindly agreed to be our accompanist until Iain's back after Christmas to direct the music again."

Everybody ooh-ed and aah-ed and started to clap, and Gabriel sat at the piano and played a flashy, tinkling, fanfare-type thing while Lynda Pym put a proprietorial hand on his shoulder and beamed down on him as if she'd invented him.

"Oi oi," one of the Year Nines commented in my ear. "Does she fancy him or what?"

"Ewww." Her mate shuddered. "That's so gross. She must be at least forty."

"You can see her point though," another remarked. "He's well fit. I'd give him one."

They dissolved into suggestively coarse cackles, and Lisa manoeuvred me away from them by my elbow. "Don't let's hang around with that lot," she murmured. "Gabriel might hear what they're saying and think we're . . . well, you know."

I did know. They weren't exactly being subtle; I was still working my way up to being gently flirty with him after his encouraging comment to me, and there was no way I wanted him to lump me in with these brazen hussies who were now grouped around him at the piano, laughing uproariously at whatever it was he was saying to them, and all but sitting in his lap.

Lynda Pym came over to us, smiling broadly. "I do believe we've got our Pink Ladies," she said with excitement. "Gabriel, would you be a darling and take these girls through their initial paces for me?"

"How do you mean, 'take us through our initial paces'?" I swallowed nervously.

"I mean sing, dear. And dance. I have to go and sort out our Sandy – she's just arrived, look. Yoo hoo, Dodie!" She waved one arm in the air like a demented loon and hurried over to the entrance, where a woman in footless tights with dyed white-blonde hair in a short urchin cut was standing in the doorway in a Notice Me kind of pose.

"Oh. My. God!" said one of the Year Nines, sniggering. "She looks about thirty. Why can't one of us be Sandy? At least we're the right age."

"Yeah! Why can't we audition?"

"The auditions were last term," said Gabriel. "So I'm guessing you lot are new to the production, are you?"

"Ooh yes baby, we're new! New and raring to go!" And they all nudged each other while Gabriel smiled tolerantly and arranged his music on the piano.

"God, just listen to them. Shameless or what?" Next to me, Lisa bristled, but I had more pressing things to think about than the Year Nines and their unsubtle attempts to chat Gabriel up.

"What do you mean, auditions?" I said. Or rather, demanded. Possibly a bit louder than I'd intended, as everyone turned to stare at me. "I didn't think anybody had to audition. I mean, that's what somebody told me," I explained in an embarrassed mutter.

"You don't have to." Gabriel smiled at me kindly. "The auditions were only for the main roles. You guys are basically the chorus, so as long as you can dance a bit, and sing more or less in tune, you'll be fine."

I opened my mouth to ask him to define "more or less", or possibly to explain about Mrs McLeish and the school choir, but closed it again sharpish. Lisa was right. Why let a bad experience when I was eight scar me for life in the singing department? Am I a victim? No, I'm not, I told myself firmly. And even if I was, the man to help heal my emotional wounds (and who knows, maybe even teach me how to sing in the process) was right there in front of me.

"Bring it on!" I said. And you know what? I actually meant it.

Amazingly, the rehearsal went really well. Despite being surrounded by the bunch of Year Nines, who tittered and primped and simpered every time Gabriel moved or breathed, I actually enjoyed myself. For Lisa, though, it seemed it hadn't so much been a rehearsal for *Grease* as a one-way ticket to paradise. Awestruck isn't the word.

"Isn't he just the most amazing person you've ever met?" she breathed. We were standing outside the church hall as everybody was leaving.

"Who, Barry? Yeah, he's cool," I said. Barry was the thirtysomething-year-old who was playing Danny Zucko. Although he was going thin on top and had a decidedly dodgy tan that made him look as if he'd been Tangoed, owing more to sunbed-worship than sunshine, he was actually pretty good. He could sing, for one thing, which I was coming to see is always helpful if you're taking part in a musical.

I meant it as a joke, but Lisa didn't even hear, so wrapped up was she in spelling out all of Gabriel's many attributes. Like I hadn't noticed them for myself.

"He's the most incredible musician, you know," she was saying. "When Dodie and Barry were singing 'Summer Nights' and it was too high, he transposed it down for them at sight. That's a really hard thing to do, you know."

"Really? Wow!"

"Absolutely. Although he could have done without those stupid girls breathing down his neck the whole time."

"You mean Starey, Drooly and Croaky?"

She laughed. "Yeah, along with Giggly and Blushy. What a bunch of losers."

Percy and Mavis-the-walnut-woman came out of the doors and said goodnight to us. "Did you have fun, girls? You seemed like you were enjoying yourselves. Will we see you again next week?"

"Oh, yes, it was brilliant," Lisa said, nodding enthusiastically. Watching them walk down the gravelled path, she turned to me again. "Do you want to come back to mine for a coffee?"

It was tempting, mainly as another excuse to dissect every single aspect of Gabriel's looks, personality, gifts and talents, etc. etc., without the Year Nines getting in the way. But I shook my head.

"Better not, I've got to catch the. . ." I trailed off as Lisa nudged me suddenly, hissing in my ear.

"Ssh! He's coming!"

Sure enough, Gabriel emerged from the doorway. At some point during the evening, Lynda Pym had produced a couple of plastic carrier bags for him to put his music in, so he wasn't quite as laden as he had been when he'd arrived.

"Hi, girls," he said, putting the carrier bags down on the ground. He took a packet of Marlboro Lights and a silver lighter from his jeans pocket, and lit up. Sam had been a smoker: it was odd, but whereas with him it was an off-putting habit, Gabriel made smoking look sexy. I know it's not, I know it's gross and stinky and gives you lung cancer, but what I'm saying is, Gabriel looked sexy doing it. Mind you, Gabriel would have looked sexy doing the housework in a pinny and a pair of Marigolds.

"Hi, Gabe." Lisa went into eyelash-batting mode. I wanted to tell her not to, that it made her appear the same as the dreaded Year Nines, but how could I? I just stood there, cringing. "How do you think that went, then?"

"The rehearsal?" Gabriel took a long drag and shrugged, blowing the smoke out through his nostrils. "It was fine. Everybody seemed to be enjoying it. That's always the main thing with these amateur dramatic wotsits."

"Yeah? Have you done much, then?"

"A bit. Hey, my dad's a vicar – I've been roped in to joining in with stuff for as long as I can remember." He looked at me. "Are you going back to Brandy Bay?"

As Brandy Bay is where I live and it was gone ten at night, I wasn't sure what he expected me to say. *No – surprise! – I'm staying with you overnight? No – surprise! – we're eloping to Gretna Green, don't you remember?* Obviously nothing of the sort. He probably just wondered if I was going back to Lisa's.

I nodded. "Yup. Actually, I'd better get a wiggle on, the last bus is in ten minutes."

Gabriel dropped his cigarette on the tarmac, and ground it out with the heel of his shoe. I recognized it as the leather mule his dog had been charging around with that afternoon we'd gone to see Bex.

His next words were so totally unexpected they left me breathless.

"I'm going that way. Fancy a lift?"

Chapter Nine

I get it now. I just assumed my life was going to be pretty much the same as most people's. You know, meet a guy, fall in love, move in together, yadda yadda – perhaps even get married and have kids one day, who knows. It's not that much to ask for, is it? But yeah. It seems like it is. Because every guy I even remotely like turns out to be a) a total bastard (e.g. Sam), b) weird (e.g. Rob), c) gay (e.g. Adam – well OK, I never found out for sure, but when a guy spends an entire hour talking about "my friend Paul", that is a bit of a giveaway), or d) uninterested/already taken.

Why the bloody hell didn't Bex tell us her bloody brother has got a girlfriend back in bloody Windsor, or wherever the bloody hell it is? By the time he dropped me off (at the top of the hill, note, because, quote, "it's such a bugger to turn round in your drive, and it's dark and I don't want to go into your wall". Wuss.) I knew everything about bloody Felicity. Her age, the colour of her hair, the subjects she's doing, what she wants to do at uni, where she wants to go to uni, her parents' names, her brothers' and sisters' names, her bloody dog's name for Chrissakes. Everything but her bra size. And I bet he'd have told me that if I'd asked.

So that's it. I'm officially giving up on men. I may as well just go off and join a nunnery.

When I arrived at school the following morning there was a bit of a to-do going on outside the sixth-form block loos. A little gossipy huddle of girls were standing outside the Ladies, all breathless with excitement. They all turned to look at me as I stopped and asked what was happening.

"It's Lisa Gray," somebody told me. "She's locked herself in one of the cubicles and won't come out."

"Why not?"

"She won't say. But she's crying her eyes out."

I could hear her the moment I pushed the door open. Crying her eyes out was about right: she was sobbing fit to bust. In fact, I wouldn't have been surprised to see a tide of salty tears coursing out from under the cubicle. I tapped uncertainly on the door.

"Lisa?" No reply. "It's me – Mattie."

A fresh burst of sobbing.

"What's wrong, hon? You can tell me."

Even more convulsive weeping. Then a weird,

indistinct, unearthly voice that sounded as if was being dragged out from a very deep place.

"Goooo 'waaaay."

"What?"

"Said, go *away*!"

No mistaking that message. I decided the way to handle the situation was to be bracing.

"I'm not going away," I told her briskly. "I'm not going anywhere. I'm staying here until you come out and tell me what's wrong, and if that means I'm here all day then that's fine by me."

Just at the point where I was beginning to wonder whether she'd taken my words at face value and we'd still be there when it got dark, the noise of her sobs juddered to a halt and eventually stopped. There was the sound of the bolt being drawn back, very slowly, and finally the door opened and Lisa emerged, blinking, as if she had been somewhere totally dark for a very long time, and the sudden light was hurting her eyes.

She looked shocking. Her face was puffy and swollen, her eyes red-rimmed, her cheeks streaked with black from her obviously non-waterproof mascara. She gave a little gasp when she saw me, and shrank back, as if I was about to leap on her and duff her up. A tiny prickle of irritation went through me, and I immediately felt guilty. Surely it's not right to feel irritated with your friends when they're as upset as she clearly was?

Ashamed of myself, I put an arm round her. "Now, what's this all about, hmm?" I cooed soothingly in her ear.

I felt her shoulders stiffen, and then she shrugged me off.

"Like you care," she muttered.

"I do care! Come on, Lis – I'm your friend!"

"Some friend." She sniffed, and turned her tear-sodden face towards me. "You knew I liked him."

"Liked. . .?" Suddenly, light dawned. "Is this about Gabriel?"

"Of *course* it's about Gabrieeel!" Her voice juddered on the last syllable of his name, like a gate catching on its hinges, and her face crumpled again. "You knew I liked him," she repeated forlornly.

It didn't seem like the right moment to remind her that, actually, I liked him too. "I know," I acknowledged, instead.

"So why did you do it?"

"Do what?" I was genuinely baffled. "What am I supposed to have done?"

"He gave you a *lift*!" she wailed. "You went in his *car* with him!"

"But . . . but that was last night." Not necessarily the response most guaranteed to pacify her, I admit, but I

132

couldn't figure out why something that happened last night was having this effect on her almost twelve hours later.

"So *what*?" She whipped her head round and faced me, her eyes blazing with something I'd never seen on her face before. Something faintly unhinged. "Aren't I allowed to be upset about it any more, then? Is there a time limit on it?"

"Well, no, of course not, but. . ." I felt slightly out of my depth. "I'm not sure why you're so upset. It was only a lift. He was going that way anyway – you must have heard him say?"

She gave a short scornful bark of a laugh. "Yeah, right! Who goes to Brandy Bay at that time of night?"

"He was going to see a mate in Luscombe. He didn't even take me all the way home, he dropped me off at the top of the hill."

"A *mate*? In *Luscombe*?" she repeated with total disbelief, as if I'd suggested he was off to indulge in a spot of badger-snogging. "He's only been living here a few weeks, how come he's suddenly got mates in Luscombe?"

"Well I don't know, do I? Perhaps it's somebody from work – didn't Bex say he's got a holiday job?" Another tingle of irritation. Why was I having to account for myself like I'd committed some kind of crime? "Honestly, Lisa. It really was only a lift. There was no hidden agenda."

"Hmph." She glared at me from under her eyebrows. At least she'd stopped weeping, although come to think of it, I wasn't sure I didn't prefer Sobbing Lisa to Accusing Lisa. "Like I said, you know how I feel about him. You didn't have to accept his lift, did you?"

"Well, no. I suppose I didn't. But. . ." *But I like him too, and I stupidly thought it might be the start of something beautiful between us?* I could hardly say that. Even though it was true. "Look, what would you have done? Given the choice between a lift from, well, practically anyone, and the mouldy old last bus to Brandy Bay?"

"But it wasn't practically anyone, was it?" she muttered mutinously. "It was Gabriel."

All at once, I'd had enough of hanging round in the loos, trying to appease her. She clearly didn't want to be appeased.

"Yes, it was Gabriel. And yes, I like him too, in case you hadn't already noticed. But that's not why I let him give me a lift home." *Liar.* I could see it on her face, but I ploughed on regardless. "And even if it was, I'd have been wasting my time because he spent the entire journey telling me about his girlfriend."

The expression on her face couldn't have been more shocked if I'd turned and punched her in the stomach. I felt a bit mean, to tell you the truth. OK, so I guess she had to know about the famous Felicity at some point, but these were possibly not the best circumstances for me to spill the beans.

"His *girlfriend*?" she whispered.

"Yeah. Back in Windsor."

She rallied slightly. "Oh. So not here in Devon, then."

"No. But I don't think it would make any difference where she is. He's obviously totally besotted. Look, I know you really like him – I do, too – but I don't think either of us is ever going to get a look-in with him."

"You think I should give up on him, you mean?" She turned her big headlamp eyes on me. "I could never do that. Laugh if you like—"

"I'm not laughing," I assured her. "Honestly. I'm just saying—"

"Laugh if you like," she repeated seriously, as if I hadn't spoken. "But if I gave up on him I'd be giving up on myself. I mean it. I may as well end my life here and now."

"So what was all that about?" Andy asked me in the kitchen at break. "All that kerfuffle outside the Ladies this morning? Jaz said you didn't get to English till half-way through second lesson."

I sighed. "Yeah. It was Lisa, she was a bit upset."

"With you?"

"No. Well, yeah." I heaved another sigh. "It's complicated."

"Don't tell me." The kettle came to the boil, and he poured water from it into two mugs. "There's got to be some lad involved."

"How did you guess?" I fiddled aimlessly with the teaspoon sticking out of the bag of sugar Andy had put on the counter. "Do you blokes get as het-up over girls as we do over you lot?"

"You're asking the wrong one, love. What would I know about that kind of thing?" He shooed me away from the sugar, heaped two teaspoons into one of the mugs, tasted it, and handed me the other. "Coffee?"

"Aw, thanks." I was touched. I was even more touched when I took a sip – it was exactly as I like it, strong but with plenty of milk and no sugar. "You're a pal, Andy."

"Yup, that's me. Everybody's pal."

There was an unusually bitter note in his voice, and I glanced at him. Was everyone in a weird mood today? "You OK?"

"Me? Course I am. Why wouldn't I be?" But it wasn't really a question. He busied himself putting the coffee things away, and I leaned against the counter and sipped at my drink. For some reason his comment had made me feel slightly uncomfortable.

"It's Bex's brother," I told him, more to break the awkward silence that had descended than anything else.

"What is?"

"The lad Lisa's got herself in a state about."

"Oh, right. Bit of a hunk, by all accounts."

"A *hunk*?" I repeated, amused. It's the kind of word girls Molly's age use to describe boys they fancy. It seemed funny to hear it on Andy's lips.

He turned round and grinned. "Yeah. A *hunk*. Got a problem with my vocabulary, have you, Miss Dictionary?"

"Do you mind?" I put my mug down and drew myself up with dignity. "It's Miss Thesaurus to you."

"Ooh-ooh!" he teased, pulling a face.

"Shut up, you!" I poked him in the ribs with a forefinger, and he doubled over with a snort of laughter. Funny, but I hadn't had him down as the ticklish type. I did it again, to the ribs on his other side, and he grabbed my wrists.

"You'll be sorry you did that, Miss Thesaurus," he said. He transferred both my wrists to one hand, and wiped his nose with the other. "Now you have to fight – the Hand of Snot!" He brandished it in my face and I squirmed away, repulsed. And, if I'm to be totally honest, rather enjoying the situation.

"No, no!" I squealed. "Not the Hand of Snot!"

"Yes, the Hand of Snot! Now beg, wench. Beg me to—"

"Ahem."

He let me go suddenly and we both wheeled round.

Jaz was standing in the kitchen entrance, looking amused. "Don't let me spoil your fun. I was only wanting the kettle."

"We were just. . ." I couldn't think what to say. It was quite clear what we were *just*. We were play-wrestling. And evidently both relishing every second. I felt the blood rush to my face, and then felt annoyed with myself. It was only *Andy*, for heaven's sake.

"Here you go." He pushed the kettle across the counter towards Jaz. "I'm done. See ya."

And he slipped past her, up the stairs to the main area.

"Bless." Jaz lifted an eyebrow, the side of her mouth raised in a sardonic little smile. "I thought you weren't interested in him."

"I'm not. It's not how it looked."

"No? Shame. You could do a lot worse. He's pretty cute, you know – I've never noticed that dimple in his chin before. And he's obviously dead keen on you."

"Yeah, *right*." I snorted. "He's not keen on me, and I'm certainly not keen on him. We were just mucking around, that's all."

"*Bonjour, mes amies!*" Bex came skipping in, beaming.

I smiled at her. "Blimey! Somebody looks happy."

"Yeah, well, I got ninety-five per cent in the French vocab test. Because I'm that cool."

"Wow! That's brilliant, well done!"

She and Jaz began to exclaim at each other in French, complete with extravagant Gallic gestures, leaving me wishing I'd kept up with the language. It would have been nice to be able to join in.

"Did you hear about Lisa?" I asked Bex, after a bit.

"I heard she locked herself in the loos this morning and wouldn't come out, and made you late for English, if that's what you mean," she said. "Why? What's she done now?"

"Oh, nothing else. I just wondered if you knew about it." I also wondered if she knew what (or rather, who) it was all about, but, knowing how she felt about stuff where her brother was involved, I didn't like to enquire further.

"Where is she now?" she asked me.

"I took her to the medical room," I told her. "She was in a right state. I thought she should go home, but she didn't want to."

"And all over your brother." Jaz clearly didn't share my concerns. She shook her head, tutting. "Madness. I mean, I know he's fit and all, but come on. No lad is worth getting in that kind of state over. If you ask me, this crush she's got on him is getting way out of hand."

"It wasn't just because of Gabriel," I put in, in the interest of fairness. "He gave me a lift home last night, after the rehearsal, and I think she thought I was mucking her around. Like I was trying to get off with him, or deliberately trying to wind her up or something."

But Jaz wasn't listening, and neither was Bex. They were off again in French, jabbering away *dix-neuf* to the *douze* about something I couldn't even begin to interpret. It gave me a strange feeling of isolation, and crossness at being ignored, and resentment at them not being interested in what I was saying, all jumbled together in an unpleasant, unfamiliar stew of emotions.

When school finished for the day Lisa was standing outside the sixth-form block, leaning against the wall, her jacket draped over her folded arms. She was obviously waiting for me, because she detached herself from the wall when she saw me coming down the stairs and stood at their foot, smiling at me. At least she looked more compos mentis than when I'd last seen her.

"Hiya," she said, and smiled again.

"You look better," I told her. "How're you feeling?"

"Fine. Well, no – not fine," she confessed. "Embarrassed, to tell you the truth. I'm really sorry I was so stupid earlier."

"No need to be embarrassed. Have you been in the medical room all day?"

"Mm-hmm. I thought somebody was going to come in and tell me to stop skiving and get to lessons, but nobody did. It was quite helpful, actually. Gave me some thinking time."

"And did you come to any conclusions?"

"Yeah. That I need my sleep." She gave a wry little laugh. "That's mainly why I was – you know. Off my head this morning. I didn't get any sleep last night, I just kept lying there, going over and over things in my brain. Daft really. Like that's going to make Gabriel like me."

"It's not daft," I murmured. I could hardly say anything about hopeless devotion to lads, could I? Look at me with Sam, less than a year ago. "We've all had crushes, you know."

"Well, anyway. Sorry for having a go at you. Why don't we go somewhere and have a snack or something? My treat."

So we went to McDonald's. And surprise, surprise – who should be serving behind the counter but. . .

"Oh heck. I totally forgot he worked here," Lisa said, standing in the doorway, blushing and nudging me. "You go and order, and I'll grab a table."

I didn't entirely believe she'd forgotten Gabriel worked there, but at least she'd stopped coming on to him like Mata Hari. I supposed I ought to be thankful for small mercies. And the place was so busy with the after-school crowd that I'm not even sure he noticed me standing patiently in the queue two away from his own. He certainly didn't notice Lisa sitting near the back.

When I got to back to her with the McCoffees she was sitting at the table she'd bagged with her chin in her hand, staring at him with a moonstruck look on her face.

"You know," she said dreamily, "he is the most beautiful person I've ever met. I feel such a connection with him. We're destined to be together, I just know we are."

"Lisa," I said warningly, "don't start all that again. He's taken, remember?"

She shrugged dismissively. "But she's still there, isn't she? In Watford."

"Windsor," I corrected her.

Another shrug. "Whatever. She's still there. And Gabriel's here. With me."

Chapter Ten

One of the main things about the Fry household nowadays – since it became the Fry-Horton household – is that we never seem to have the opportunity to sit down together to chat about stuff. In the old days, BG (Before Geoffrey), Mum and Molly and me used to eat together most nights, and certainly on the weekends. Occasionally, and when Mum said the funds would allow, we'd go to the Black Dog at Combe Bridge, or the Admiral Benslow at Luscombe if she was especially flush, for Sunday lunch. We'd use these eating-together times not just to eat but to keep each other up-to-date with what was going on in our respective lives, as well as just general nattering about Life, the Universe and Everything. I'd thought all families sat around a gingham-tableclothed table every evening, telling each other what kind of day they'd had. I'd thought it was what families did. (I realize all this might make us sound vomit-inducingly like the Waltons, but it's just how things were.)

I don't know when I realized that we'd stopped doing it. It must have been some time ago, though, because when Mum announced out of the blue that we were all going out to lunch on Sunday, Moll and I looked at each other in a what-brought-that-on kind of way.

"That's nice," said Moll, brightly.

I raised an eyebrow. "How come?"

"What do you mean, 'how come'?" Mum asked.

"I mean, why are we all suddenly going out to lunch? We never go out to lunch."

"Exactly. That's why we're going." Mum gave a tinkling little laugh that somehow didn't ring true. Definitely suss, then. "We just thought it would be nice. We never seem to sit down and eat together as a family these days."

"That could be because Rupert isn't here most of the time."

Rupert, in case you've been wondering, is considered Too Clever for St Mark's (Too Clever By Half, if you ask me), and boards during the week at a school over the border in Somerset, where he's on some kind of Gifted and Talented programme.

"He's here at weekends," Moll pointed out. "And during the holidays. I think it's a great idea, Mum. Thanks."

And she gave her a big hug, which struck me as being way over the top. I mean, come on. It was only

Sunday lunch being proposed, not a Caribbean cruise. And Sunday lunch with Gomez and Pugsley Addams, to boot. What a treat.

"So where are we going?" I muttered. I sounded ungracious even to my own ears – Lisa's increasing weirdness about Gabriel had been preying on my mind all weekend – but Mum didn't pick up on it.

"We thought the Admiral Benslow," she said, smiling. "They do a nice roast on Sundays, and the veggie options are pretty good, too. I had a fabulous butternut squash risotto the last time Geoffrey and I were there."

I stared at her. I hadn't realized Mum and Geoffy Baby had been sneaking off to the Benslow behind our backs. "When was that, then?"

"I can't remember, exactly. A couple of weeks ago?" She smiled again. "Don't look like that, darling. Geoffrey and I do have a life of our own outside of this house. We work at the same institution so of course we have lunch together from time to time!"

"I *know*," I replied, irritably. I did know – of course I did. They were two grown-up people, married to each other. Why shouldn't they have lunch together? Why shouldn't they do stuff I knew nothing about? And why was I feeling so uneasy about this whole Sunday Lunch thing?

*

I didn't have to wait long to find out. No sooner were we all seated at our reserved table and flicking through the huge leatherette-bound menus with "Admiral Benslow Restaurant and Grill" in fancy gold blocking on their fronts, than Geoffrey cleared his throat in an I'm-going-to-make-an-announcement kind of manner. The rest of us looked up expectantly. The rest of us, that is, apart from Mum, who continued to toy with her orange juice whilst staring into the middle distance with a vague, dreamy look on her face.

"There is a reason. . ." He cleared his throat again, nervously. "We're not just here for. . . The reason we . . . ahem. The thing is. . ." He trailed off helplessly. *Blimey*, I thought. *Imagine being at a lecture given by him. You'd fall asleep way before he got to the point.*

Mum dragged her attention back to the table. She put a hand over his and patted it, kindly. "What Geoffrey is trying to say. . ." she began.

I nudged Moll with my elbow. "Here we go," I whispered. She kicked me on the ankle in response, and glared at me.

"It's quite simple really," Mum was saying. "Geoffrey has been very worried about telling you children, but I'm sure you'll be as thrilled at the news as we are. At least, I hope you will be." She took a slow, careful sip of her drink. "What Geoffrey was trying to say is . . . we're going to have a baby."

I was still bristling at the "you children" bit of her little speech, so it took a moment or two for the rest of what she'd said – the thrust of it, as it were – to sink in. When it did, I surprised even myself by my response.

"Hey," I exclaimed. I could feel my mouth turning itself upwards in an approximation of a smile. Whether it reached my eyes, I didn't know. "That's really cool." I glanced down at the menu again, the words blurring on the page. "I must just go to the loo. If they come for our order before I'm back, I'll have the roast, erm, pork."

Inside the sanctuary of the Ladies I locked myself in a cubicle and lowered myself on to the seat, the lid still down. Roast *pork*? What was I thinking? I hate roast pork. Never eat the stuff. Something to do with the crackling, the poor dead pig's fat and skin, invariably with a few sad stiff bristles still attached. . . I hardly ever ate veggie any more, hadn't really done so since Geoffrey and Rupert came into our lives, but my distaste for roast pork was obviously a hangover of my vegetarian upbringing.

Geoffrey and Rupert. I gulped. And now there was to be another Horton, a little—

The door to the Ladies opened with a crash, and a voice called my name.

"Mat? Are you in there?" It was Molly. She rapped on the door.

"Sssh," I replied, crossly. "Shut up."

"Why? I just wanted to make sure you're OK."

"I don't want to discuss our family business in here. It's not the place."

"It's all right. There's nobody else here."

Slowly, I got up from the toilet and unbolted the door. Even more slowly, I stepped out from the cubicle. Molly was standing by the hand drier, looking apprehensive. She was right: all the other doors stood open. We were alone.

"Phew." I let out my breath in a loud exhalation. "Bit of a toughie, that."

"Yeah. Trust Mum and Geoffrey to think the right place to tell us the glad tidings was in a crowded pub."

"It's not a pub," I corrected her. "It's a *restaurant*. As they keep reminding all and sundry."

She grinned, clearly glad I was taking it so well. Lucky she couldn't see the thoughts that were thronging my brain.

"Did you see Rupert's face? He looked like one of those whole salmon they have on the fish bit at Sainsbury's. It was worth it just to see him look like that."

"You reckon?" I said, grimly.

"Maybe not." She took a step towards me and touched my arm. "Look, Mat, I know it's been a shock for you, but—"

"A shock for *me*? Why just me? I'd have thought it

was a shock for all of us." I looked into her face suspiciously. "You didn't already know, did you?"

She coloured up, the blush spreading quickly across her cheeks. "Yes. Well, no. Not exactly. I guessed."

"You *guessed*? How? Mum said, 'Let's all go out for Sunday lunch' and you thought, 'Hey, I know, they're going to tell us she's pregnant'?"

"Course not." She snorted. "I'm not a clairvoyant, am I?"

"Woah. Big word," I said with sarcasm.

Molly took a deep breath. "I know it's been a shock," she repeated calmly, "but it's no use taking it out on me. I only guessed because I've overheard Mum and Geoffrey discussing . . . stuff."

"What kind of stuff?"

"Baby stuff. Buying pushchairs over the internet. Babies' names. That kind of stuff."

"Oh sweet Jesus," I groaned.

"I know. It makes it real, doesn't it? It took me a while to get my head round it, too."

"So why didn't you tell me?"

"I did think about it. But then I thought, well, it's not my news to tell, is it? And what if I'd been wrong? What if I'd put two and two together and come up with twenty-two? Anyway, if I was right, I knew they'd tell us eventually. They'd have to. So I thought it was best to let them do it, in their own time."

"And their own time is obviously now." I turned the cold tap on and ran my wrists underneath the stream of water. It was cool and clear. Unlike my thought processes. "Don't you think it's kind of. . .?" I couldn't think of the right word, pulled a face instead, and shuddered.

"Minging?" Molly shrugged. "A bit. I mean, Mum's turned forty, hasn't she? There must be risks. She's probably going to have to do all those tests and things. Gross-out."

I hadn't meant that. I'd been thinking more that this baby – this *embryo*, growing inside Mum now, this very moment, as my sister and I were standing discussing it – was the clearest possible proof that our mother and stepfather. . . I couldn't finish the thought, even inside my own head.

"And apart from all that, it obviously means they've been having sex," Moll piped up.

"Eww! Too much information." I pulled another face, even more distasteful than the last.

"Well, it does, doesn't it? That's probably why Rupert had his Dead Fish face on him. But I tell you what. . ." She obligingly pulled a handful of tissues from the box by the mirror and passed them to me. Bless. She knows I hate those hot air thingies.

"What?" I started carefully dabbing at my hands.

"We're going to have to get used to the idea. All

three of us. 'Cos this baby's not going to go away, is it?"

When Moll and I returned to the table there was an opened bottle of white wine sitting on it, and a full glass of it by my place. The food had not only been ordered but had arrived already, and soothing classical music was playing quietly in the background, just below the gentle hubbub of the diners' chit-chat. Rupert and Geoffrey were deep in conversation about God knows what, which Molly immediately joined in as she slid into her seat.

I looked at my plate. Whatever was on it, it didn't look like pork.

"It's chicken," Mum told me from across the table. I glanced at her, surprised, and she smiled anxiously. "I know you said pork, but I thought you probably meant chicken."

"Yeah, I did actually. Thanks." I picked up my wine glass and took a long swig. Boy, did I need it. "Mm, this is nice."

"Is it? It's an Australian Chardonnay. Geoffrey ordered it. You know me, I don't know anything about wine."

"Yeah, you do. You know you get pissed from just one sniff of the cork." I smiled at her, making an effort, and as she smiled back the anxiety left her eyes and was replaced by something else. It was probably relief, but it looked like gratitude.

So, how was I left feeling about the prospect of having another sibling join the happy Fry-Horton clan? As if I'd been hit by a ten-tonne truck just about covers it. Well, how would you feel, under the circumstances? OK, so in terms of world disasters it wasn't exactly up there with hurricanes and earthquakes, I realize that. I mean, nobody died. But it was still pretty earth-shattering to me.

Mum and Geoffrey, producing a child: there were so many implications. It would share their genes. More scarily, it would share mine and Rupert's, too, or at least some of them. Would Mum be able to cope? Would she carry on working after it was born? Where would it sleep? *Would* it sleep? Would it let *us* sleep? Everybody knows babies make a din, would it wake us all (OK, me) up at night? And the thing that possibly overshadowed everything else – would Mum love it more than Moll and me? I know, I know. It makes me sound about four years old. But think about it. Mum and Dad split up years ago, they never got on, he used to beat her up, and here she was now, expecting a baby with a man she loved (I'm trying to suspend disbelief here; he's not exactly my idea of Mr Wonderful but hey, he's her choice) . . . whose child was she more likely to cherish? I'm not proud of thinking it, but I couldn't help it.

The thoughts bubbled away in my brain until they were literally doing my head in. I had to share them with somebody or I thought the top of my skull might actually explode. Under normal circumstances I'd have been round to Jaz's like a shot, but they were hardly normal circumstances. It's not every day you tell your best mate that your stepfather and forty-year-old mother have, ahem, made a baby. What if she was disgusted? What if she thought I was kidding around? What if – and this would be worst of all – she *laughed*?

In the end I didn't go round, but rang her instead. The phone was picked up on the first ring.

"Hello?" Her brother.

"Oh hi, Surjit. It's Mattie. Blimey, that was quick! Were you standing by the phone?"

"Just walking past it, babe. You want Jasmilla, yeah? Sorry, but she's out."

My heart sank. I so needed to talk to her. "Oh."

"Try her moby. You'll always get her on that."

"I can't. It's really expensive."

"Oh, aren't you with Virgin? Yeah, it's not cheap to ring other networks. . . Listen babe, I gotta go. I'll tell her you rang, shall I?"

Useless to explain that I still lived in the Dark Ages and didn't possess a mobile, and that Mum had forbidden me to ring Jaz's – or anybody else's – mobile from our phone on pain of death (just a hunch, but the hundred pounds-plus bill I'd run up a year back doing just that might have had something to do with it. . .). Pregnant elderly mother, no mobile – I was beginning to feel like a proper freak.

So I just muttered yeah, and thanks, and hung up.

And then I thought, stuff it. Why shouldn't I ring Jaz on her mobile? This was an emergency. I didn't have to spend long on the phone. I could even ask her to call me back. Whatever. I had, had, HAD to speak with her. . .

So. Her phone rang and rang. And rang. And then: *Hey. This is Jaz. Leave a message.* Frustrated beyond belief, practically crying with disappointment, I slammed the phone back down on its cradle. But no sooner had I done so than it rang suddenly, making me jump. I snatched it up.

"Hello?"

"Mattie? It's me."

"Oh, Jaz, hi! Oh, thank goodness it's you! I was trying to ring you but I got your voicemail."

"I know. I had it on silent alert, I saw it was you on missed messages. What's up?"

"How long have you got?" I laughed shortly.

"Well . . . erm, not long, actually. Are you in trouble?"

"Trouble? No. I just wanted to bend your ear."

"Aah." A long pause. "Can it possibly wait till school tomorrow?"

I had the strangest sensation in my stomach. A sort of lurch – the kind you get going too fast over a hump-backed bridge.

"Er, yeah. I guess. Why – what are you doing?"

"I'm at the arts centre in Luscombe. They're showing a classic French movie, it's just about to start. I've bought the ticket and everything."

"Oh, right." I did some fast thinking. "Well, look, how about you come over here after it's finished? It's only seven o'clock – you could be here by, what, ten-ish? You could even stay over, I'm sure Mum would be OK with that." She'd have to be, I thought grimly. I reckoned she owed me one after taking her little bombshell so well earlier. "I can even dig out a toothbrush for you. There's a spare one in the bathroom." Another silence. "Are you still there?"

"Erm . . . yeah. I'm still here. The thing is. . ." Her voice became indistinct, underwatery, as if she'd put her hand over the phone to speak to somebody else. Then it came back again. "The thing is, I can't really. I'm going on somewhere else afterwards. I'm really sorry, Mat. But we'll talk about whatever it is tomorrow, I promise. OK?"

"OK." It was unlike Jaz to stay out late on a Sunday

night: she was always so conscientious about getting homework done and having an early night before school the next day. "Where are you going, then – afterwards?"

"It's, erm, a sleepover, actually."

"Oh." Since when did Jaz have sleepovers with anybody apart from me? Something else occurred to me. "So have you gone to see this film by yourself?"

"No. That's the point. I'm here with Bex. That's where I'm going afterwards. Back to hers."

Chapter Eleven

The odd thing was, Jaz didn't seem to think there was anything out of the ordinary about going to anybody else's for a sleepover. I say odd, but it was actually quite upsetting. Especially when I went up to the sixth-form block at break on Monday and the first people I saw were her and Bex. Nothing wrong with that, except the two of them were standing in a corner by the window, their heads inclined towards each other, deep in conversation. I dithered. Should I go over and talk to them? That old cliché about three being a crowd ran through my mind, but before I could decide what to do Jaz threw her head back and laughed, a rich hearty guffaw that made up my mind for me. I'd never heard her laugh that way before with anybody other than me. I pinned a cheery and phony smile on my face, and strode over.

"Morning, morning! And how are we all today?" God. I was turning into Geoffrey. I was even rubbing my hands together in that convivial manner of his. Scary. . .

"Hey." Bex turned her head in my direction and smiled languidly. "How you doing?"

"Yeah, I'm good." In which case, why was I gurning like a goon? "How was the film?"

She just smiled again, non-committally.

"It was fab," Jaz replied instead. "Shame you're not doing French. You could have come too."

"Yeah," I agreed. It did cross my mind to ask if I could have come with her to the overnighter at Bex's as well. But I didn't. Of course I didn't.

"Shan't be a minute," Bex said suddenly. "I must just go and have a word with. . ." And she waved a vague hand and drifted off.

"So it was good, then?" I said to Jaz. "The film? Your evening?"

She gave me a slightly strange look. *I just said so, didn't I?* "The film was good, yeah."

"And?" I prompted her.

The strange look intensified. "And what?"

"And the rest of your evening. The sleepover. How was that?"

"It was cool."

"So what did you do?"

"Ate some pizza, drank some Fanta, did some French homework, crashed out on Bex's floor." She regarded me levelly. "I went back to hers afterwards so we could write up our French coursework notes together. I only stayed over because we knew it would be late before we finished, and I didn't think it was fair to get Dad to turn out after midnight to pick me up."

I felt guilty, as if I'd been caught out spying on her. I put a hand on her arm. "It's OK. You don't have to tell me all this."

"Don't I?"

"Of course not! You can do what you want to, you don't have to explain yourself to me."

"I know I don't *have* to. I just got the feeling—" She stopped abruptly and shrugged. "Never mind. Listen, why don't we do something together on Saturday afternoon? Go into town, or something?"

"Oh, I can't!" I was genuinely disappointed. "I promised Lisa I'd go shopping with her. She wants to buy a new top."

Her face hardened, and she pressed her lips together in a smile that stopped way short of her eyes.

"OK. Fine. Some other time, perhaps. Look, I need to get to German early today. Catch up with you later, yeah?"

She hurried off, and it was only after she'd gone clacking up the stairs in her kitten heels that I realized I still hadn't told her about Mum and Geoffrey and the baby.

*

It soon became obvious that when Lisa had said she wanted to buy a new top, what she actually meant was that she wanted to go round every single clothes shop in Luscombe, cart gazillions of tops into the fitting room, make me wait outside the curtain while she modelled every single one for me, go on to the next shop where ditto, and end up, what felt like weeks later, back at the first shop – where she bought the very first top she'd tried on. Now, I like shopping as much as the next girl, but it was knackering. Maybe because for me it wasn't so much shopping as observing.

Once she'd finally made her choice – black and red, corset-stylee, low-cut, foxy – and had paid for it and was bearing it out of the shop in its smart, thick, card bag with knotted rope handles (it was that kind of shop), she turned to me.

"I'm shattered. Shall we go and have a drink?"

"What? But I haven't had a chance to look for anything yet!"

She groaned. "I know, but I'm just sooo tired. My feet are killing me. Let's go to Clarrie's and have a coffee and a sticky cake, shall we? They do the best chocolate éclairs, have you ever had them?"

Lisa was right, the éclairs were fabulous; which was just as well after the morning I'd had with her. Even though she changed her mind at the last moment and had a diet Coke rather than a coffee, and didn't touch the pastries when they came.

"You have them," she told me. "I'm not that hungry any more. The bubbles in Coke always fill me up, don't you find that?"

"Nope. I can always eat cream cakes," I said, reaching for the second éclair. "Are you sure you don't want this?"

"No, it's OK. I don't know why I ordered it. I've put on so much weight lately – didn't you notice how fat I looked in most of those tops?"

"You looked fine to me." I took a large, satisfying bite. A glob of cream escaped from the side of my mouth; I scooped it up with my little finger and popped it back in.

"I didn't. You're just being nice." She was sitting across the table from me, and drooped a little. "I'm such a glutton. I just can't resist eating."

"*You're* a glutton?" I giggled through the cream and chocolate and crumbs of choux pastry. "What d'you call me, then?"

"It's all right for you. You can take it. You're all tall and willowy and gorgeous. I'm just a big lardy blob."

I was torn between vanity, i.e. preening at the compliments (nobody had called me any of those things before), and decency, i.e. trying to reassure her that she wasn't a big lardy blob. Fortunately, decency won.

"You're not! How can you say that? OK, maybe you're not as tall as me, but you're certainly not fat."

"But I *am*," she wailed softly. She bent down and pulled the new top from its bag with a miserable little flourish. "I may as well take this back. I looked hideous in it. I don't know why I bought it."

"Oh God, no, don't do that!" I was horrified. (Does it make me sound really selfish to admit that the thought of trailing round all the shops with her for another second was making me lose the will to live? OK then: I'm selfish.) "It looked fab, honestly! You've got the figure to wear corset tops. You need proper boobs to keep them up. They just make me look like a boy."

She sighed, and shoved the top back in the bag. "Thank you for being kind, but I've got eyes. I know how hideous I look. Fat, plain and boring. No wonder Gabriel doesn't look twice at me."

"Lisa, you're not! Don't be silly!" What could I say? She wasn't fat, she wasn't plain, she wasn't boring. On the other hand, nobody could call her sylph-like, a stunner and a fascinating conversationalist. At the end of the day, she was just . . . well, ordinary. Very similar to me, in fact. A bit curvier, a bit shorter, a bit darker-haired. But ordinary. Apart from anything else, I really didn't have the energy for another Gabriel-dissecting session with her. As much to change the topic as anything else, I said, "Hey, I'll tell you somebody who's going to be properly fat before much longer. My mum. She's pregnant."

If I felt a twinge of guilt at referring to Mum like that, it was worth it. Lisa's expression changed immediately, all her self-preoccupation falling away at the scent of a bit of goss. Until the words left my mouth, I don't think I really appreciated just how much I was longing to tell somebody, anybody, about it. And despite all the shop-trawling beforehand – or maybe even because of it – Lisa fitted the bill just fine.

"Your mum's pregnant? Oh. My. God! How?" Her eyes were as big and round as saucers.

"Erm . . . the usual way, I expect. I didn't really ask her."

She giggled, and put a hand up to her mouth. "Silly! I didn't mean *how* how, I meant. . . Well, I guess I meant how far gone is she. When's it due?"

I shrugged, nonchalantly. "No idea. I didn't ask her that, either."

"You mean, you don't know when your little brother or sister is going to be born?" She was clearly shocked. "Oh. I think I'd want to know."

"Why would I want to know that? I just thank Christ she's not showing yet. Did you know that in the olden days, pregnant women had to stay indoors so nobody could see them? I think I might start a movement to bring that back. Starting with my mother."

"You don't mean that!" She laughed, then looked at my face. "Oh dear. You do mean it. You're upset about it, aren't you?"

"You could say that, yeah." I was suddenly embarrassed at having told her. I picked up my coffee cup and drained it to the dregs, even though it had gone stone-cold long since.

"Is your sister upset about it as well? Is that why she was crying at school the other day?"

"Was she?" I blinked, startled. "How do you know that?"

"I saw her. She was in the corridor outside the library with that friend of hers. You know, the pretty blonde one?"

"Chloë."

"That's right. Chloë. She was in a right old state. Molly, I mean, not Chloë."

"Why, what was she doing?" It didn't sound like Moll to me.

"Crying, like I said. Sobbing her heart out. She had mascara all streaked down her cheeks."

"*Mascara*?" Since when did my little sister wear make-up to school? "Are you sure?"

"Of course I'm sure. She looked like a panda. She ought to get some good waterproof stuff – I know it's a total pain to get off at night, you need those special eye make-up remover pads, but it's worth it. I got a good one just the other day, look. . ." And she rooted around in her make-up bag.

I flapped an irritated hand at her. "Never mind that. I meant, are you sure it was Molly? She doesn't usually do public displays of crying." In point of fact, she doesn't usually do private ones, either. Much as it pains me to admit it, of the two of us I'm the one with the tendency for diva moments. Moll's usually the calm, rational, reasonable one.

"Of course I'm sure it was her! I was as close to her as – well, as I am to you now."

"So did you say anything to her?"

"Well, no. Her friend had her arm round her and seemed to be coping OK, so I thought it was better to just leave her to it." She leaned towards me across the table, concerned. "So wasn't it about your mum and the baby, then? The reason she was upset?"

"I don't know. I don't think so. She hasn't seemed upset about it with me." Or about anything else, for that matter. I wondered what was going on. Perhaps I ought to ask Molly about it when I got home.

Lisa leaned even further across the table. "But you're upset, I can see that. Do you want to talk about it?" Her expression was solicitous, her voice kindly. It was tempting. But I felt I'd said more than enough and when all was said and done, we were sitting in a crowded teashop. If I stretched my arms out I could probably touch about five other people on different tables. None of whom I especially wanted to share my innermost feelings with.

I shrank back slightly, pulling a face. "Not really. It's a bit, erm. . ." I looked round meaningfully.

Lisa cottoned on immediately. "Oh, right. I get you. Well, why not come back to mine, then? I mean, I've finished my shopping, and you didn't want to get anything, did you?"

Slightly to my surprise, Lisa lived in one of the big white-painted houses set up above the harbour in Combe Bridge. And when I say big, I mean BIG. The ground floor rooms all opened off a large central hallway with a huge sweeping staircase, the kind the top-hatted-and-tailed cast dance down in musicals. There was a huge farmhouse-style kitchen and a TV room and study, and not one downstairs loo but two, one of which was a shower room as well. You could get lost in her sitting room. It had gigantic picture windows, front and rear, one opening up on to the equally gigantic back garden (vast expanses of tidily manicured green lawn, neatly-weeded flowerbeds, shrubs and mature trees, backing on to the open fields beyond), the other with an extremely fetching view over the harbour. The kind of fetching view that, together with the house's dimensions and other "desirable features", to come over all estate-agency about it, would probably bring in around a cool mil should Lisa's parents decide to put it on the market right now.

I'm not sure why the fact that Lisa lived in a mini-mansion surprised me. Probably because she's not all snooty and snobby like some other girls at school from well-off families, who shove it in your face at every conceivable opportunity: *ooh, look at my new mobile, I had the last one for a whole month and got fed-up with it – my Daddy's just got promoted and he's taking us all to lunch at the weekend. In London – we're going to the Caribbean for our summer holidays. For a month.* Grrr. Don't get me started. (And yes, I admit it: it's probably just jealousy.) But there's a real mix of backgrounds at St Mark's, from the offspring of generations of fishermen and farmers, to the wealthy London businessmen who only come down at weekends and whose families, like Lisa's, live in the large houses scattered above the harbour, built in the 1920s and 30s as holiday homes for the filthy rich.

Lisa's bedroom, prettily decorated in pinks and mauves and lilacs, was the size of the entire downstairs of our cottage. The centre of the room was dominated by an enormous king-size bed, covered with a baby-pink satin comforter heaped about with mounds of differently sized and shaped cushions, and festooned with pink-and-cream gauze drapes that were suspended from a gold-painted coronet on the ceiling above. Similar swathes of fabric were draped around the large bay window that overlooked the garden. The whole effect was frou-frou and girly, and way over the top.

"Hey!" I exclaimed. I put my hands on my hips and surveyed it all with approval. "I'm loving your room!"

Lisa wrinkled her nose slightly. "Thanks. I've outgrown all that little-girl, princess stuff, to be honest. Mum had it done for me when I was ten, and it cost a bomb. As she never stopped reminding me. I think she'd throw a total mental if I asked to have it redecorated."

"But you're sixteen now," I pointed out.

"Seventeen," she corrected me. "Last month."

A small pang of guilt passed through me, that I hadn't known, hadn't given her a birthday card. But only a small pang. How could I have known it was her birthday unless she told me?

I shrugged. "The point is, you're not a little girl any more. If you want something more, I dunno, sophisticated, that's up to you. Right?"

"You know that, I know that. Mum's view is that I should be grateful for stuff for my whole life." She gave an apologetic little laugh. "Which I am, of course I am. I love it really."

"What about brothers and sisters? Have you got any?"

"Two brothers. Half-brothers," she amended. "Same dad, different mum. They're grown-up – in their late twenties. I hardly ever see them."

"Shame. I was thinking you might get them to stick up for you. You know, remind them that Lisa's all grown up now and doesn't want to live in Barbie's enchanted castle for ever."

"That would be cool, wouldn't it? But it's not going to happen. And I don't think it would have any effect even if it did. My mum's father was ill for years and couldn't work, and she grew up without much money to spare. She still acts as though she's living in poverty, God knows why – she's a total skinflint, it drives my father bonkers."

"What does he do?"

"He's a pilot."

"Cool!" Suddenly Lisa's homely, ordinary features took on a different air, a kind of over-glow of glamour. "What, down at Heathrow?"

"No. At Charles de Gaulle. Paris," she explained, seeing my look of bafflement.

"Wow!" I was, for once in my life, lost for words. "Just – *wow*!"

She gave me a look, slightly askance. "It's not that great, you know. It means when he's not flying to

Sydney, or LA, or – or bloody *Timbuktu*, he's in France. I hardly ever get to see him. Listen, d'you think Jaz fancies Gabriel?"

The sudden change of subject took me by surprise. "What?"

"Jaz. Does she fancy him?"

"Why ask me?" Even when I said the words the alternative, more accurate answer – *no way* – was running through my brain. I still don't know why I didn't just say that.

"You're her mate. I guess I thought she'd have told you."

Our eyes met, and for a fraction of a second I hesitated. Even though I knew I should have just been truthful and explained that, for the moment at any rate, Jaz's heart belonged to Patrice.

"It would explain a lot, wouldn't it?" I said instead.

"Like, why is Bex suddenly her new best friend?"

I would have stuck up for Jaz, but I didn't get the chance. Lisa was standing in the middle of the room, her face working slightly like a small child about to burst into tears. Then she threw herself down on the shiny pink bedspread.

"I think I would die," she began, slowly, unevenly, "if Gabriel fancied her back."

This was starting to go too far. "No, you wouldn't," I said. I went over and perched on the side of the bed, next to her. "You wouldn't actually die. Come on, Lisa!"

"I would. If they started dating, I would die. Of a broken heart. She's just everything I'm not, isn't she?" She picked up a heart-shaped pink-and-white gingham cushion with the word "Babydoll" embroidered in fancy lettering across its front, and hugged it to her chest. "She's smart. Funny. Drop-dead gorgeous. And *thin*." The last word ended on a kind of wail, and she buried her face in the cushion while I sat there next to her, not knowing quite what to say.

"Don't be so hard on yourself." I patted her shoulder ineffectually. "You've got really great qualities too. Come on – think positive!"

"The thing is. . ." she began in a muffled, mournful voice. She raised her head from the cushion and looked at me, her eyes rimmed with red, like a white rabbit's. I noticed for the first time that they weren't any particular colour – greyish, blueish. Nothing-coloured eyes. "The thing is . . . I love him. I adore him. He's the man for me, the one I want to spend the rest of my life with. I just know he is."

Well, how could I answer that? *No, he's not, because he's only nineteen and you're only seventeen and how can you possibly know that kind of thing at your age? No, he's not, he's already got a girlfriend? No, he's not, because actually I still fancy him myself, and I'll fight you to the death for him, so how about pistols at dawn?* Hardly. Besides, I didn't get the chance to answer, because she suddenly thrust the cushion to one side, swung her feet over the edge of the bed and stood up.

"I must go to the loo," she said, her voice still wobbling slightly. "Shan't be long."

While she was gone, I aimlessly flicked my eyes over her things. She had her own landline phone on the bedside table, I noticed: pale cream, the old-fashioned candlestick-shaped type with an earpiece that sits hooked over the bit you speak into. Class. I wandered over to her dressing table, which was strewn with make-up and various bits of expensive-looking jewellery and miniature scent samples: Chanel, Dior, Thierry Mugler, Jean-Paul Gaultier. Souvenirs from her dad's duty-free airport travels, no doubt.

Then I saw it. Sitting innocently on the dressing table, in between a silver-backed hairbrush and a pot of candyfloss-pink lipgloss. A small volume bound with red leather, no bigger than a paperback book, with four numbers printed in a tiny silver font on the front: this year's date. It was Lisa's diary.

Now, I know all about personal space, and privacy. I went ape when Geoffrey and Rupert moved in with us and Moll and I had to start sharing a room. I'm paranoid about anybody finding my own diary and reading it unsupervised. Despite the fact it's the kind with a miniature padlock, I change its hiding place regularly in case anybody susses where I keep it. I'm even not totally over the shock of when I accidentally stumbled across Rupert's online diary, some time ago now, and was confronted with the unpleasant truth of what he really thought about me.

I knew all of this, plus what an abuse of trust and friendship it is to sneakily read somebody else's diary. It was sheer nosiness that made me do it. Nosiness, plus opportunity. It's no excuse, I know – I'm still ashamed of myself for it.

I picked up Lisa's diary, opened it at random, and began to read.

Chapter Twelve

Bloody hellfire. I should NOT have read that. What came over me? I don't want to know that Lisa's turning into a stalker. Who writes long love-letters to Gabriel that she never posts, who walks up and down the road outside the vicarage for hours on end, hoping to catch a glimpse of him. Who's been going into Maccy D's pretty much every day after school and has worked out his shift pattern. Who's totally convinced herself that Jaz and Gabriel fancy each other and Jaz is trying to worm her way into his life – not to mention his pants – by being all über-matey with Bex, and that she (L) wants to kill her (J) every time she claps eyes on her. She actually wants to do her physical damage. She admitted it.

And I CERTAINLY didn't want to know that she's convinced herself the only reason Gabriel doesn't fancy her is because she's a fat ugly waste of space, and she's started making herself throw up after eating. I so didn't want to know that. . .

So what am I supposed to do with all this knowledge?

*I STILL haven't really spoken to anybody about Mum being
pregnant, and now there's all this heavy stuff about Lisa, too.
I had no idea she was hiding so much. And now I do know,
what am I supposed to do with it? Just carry it all around
with me?*

   Shit.

   Help!

   SHIT!!!!!!!!!!

One thing I did do, though, was ask Moll about the
crying, although, predictably, she denied it.

"Crying?" she said. "Outside the school library?" She
wrinkled her nose, made a face of baffled trying-to-
recollect. Like she'd have forgotten it. "When was this
supposed to have been, then?"

"I'm not sure. She didn't actually say."

"She?" She pounced. "Who's *she*?"

"Lisa," I said, trying to remain patient. "It was Lisa
who told me about it. I did say. Lisa saw you and Chloë
outside the library, and she thought it looked like you
were in tears."

"Well, she was wrong." Molly's face turned from
baffled to mutinous, and my patience deserted me.

"Come on, Moll. Don't pretend. Lisa said you were
in bits. Are you saying she's telling lies?"

Molly just shrugged. "Dunno."

"It's Mum, isn't it?"

"What is?"

"What you were upset about. It's Mum, and this flippin' baby thing."

"It's not a baby *thing*. It's a baby. And for your information, no, I'm not upset about that. In fact, if you want to know the truth, I'm quite looking forward to it. Now, if that's all. . ." She turned her back on me haughtily. "I've got homework to do."

And that, it appeared, was that. *Well, I'm upset about it,* I wanted to say. Wanted to wail. I wanted to grab her by the sleeve and bury my head in the crook of her arm, and wail. *I'm dead upset about it, and I've got nobody to talk to!* But how could I do that? I'm Moll's big sister, not the other way round.

Pathetic. That's what I am at times. Pathetic.

Oddly enough, it was Andy I told. About everything. It's not like I planned to. I was walking across the playground after lunch on my way to the library, my arms full of books, and Andy came flying out of the door to the boys' changing rooms and nearly ran slap-bang into me. As it was, he clipped my left elbow. I spun round, all the books crashing to the wet tarmac below.

"Bloody hell! Mattie, I'm really sorry." He bent down on one knee to retrieve the books, and when he handed them up to me, still semi-kneeling, I was surprised to see how red his face was. He seemed really flustered. Poor bloke – I thought I was the only one who got embarrassed when I thought I'd made a public idiot of myself.

"Don't worry about it, they're only library books." I gave him a reassuring smile, and leaned in towards him to take them just as he got to his feet. Our heads narrowly avoided colliding, and I took a half-step backwards.

"Oops!" I laughed. "Steady on! I've heard of being swept off your feet, but this is ridiculous!" He didn't reply properly, just mumbled something inaudible and blushed again, the dull crimson sweeping across his jawline like a stain.

"Hey, did I tell you about my mum?" I chirped brightly, more as a way of distracting him from his embarrassment than because I'd had any previous intentions of sharing my family secrets with him.

It did the trick. "Your mum? No," he said, his face taking on a concerned expression: interested, but not too prying.

I told him as we walked to the library together, and if I'd been surprised by his girly blushes then his rapt attention as I rambled on about Mum and Geoffrey and the baby, and then about Lisa, took me even more by surprise. Nice bloke and everything, but I'd never had him down as a good listener. But he was. A surprisingly wise one, too.

"You know what I think? It's natural you should feel confused about this baby."

I opened my mouth to say *I'm not confused*, but closed it again when I realized he was right. Confusion was exactly what I'd been feeling.

"You think so?" I said instead.

"God, yeah. I mean, a new baby, made by your mum and her old man – it's going to be all oochy-coochy-coo, isn't it?"

"Yeah," I said grimly. "Precisely what I've been thinking. If there's one thing I can't stand, it's all that soppy baby-talk stuff."

"But she's still going to be your mum, isn't she? And you're still her daughter. No amount of new babies will change that."

"I guess not." Andy was right, of course. But there was still the matter of. . .

"Course, it's going to be your own flesh and blood, but at the same time it's proof your mum and wotsisname have been at it, isn't it? *Way* embarrassing."

Trust Andy to get right down to the nitty-gritty. Just like Moll had, before. But again, he was right.

"That's it, exactly! How did you know how I was feeling?"

He shrugged. "Lucky guess. Plus it's exactly how I was feeling this time last year. My sister was having a baby with her partner – he's a bit of a knob to be honest, a waste of space in my opinion, but she seems happy enough with him. I kept telling myself it was going to be my niece or nephew, but all I could see in my mind was this little kid with Knobhead's face staring up at me."

Geoffy Baby. . .

"So. . .?" I held out my hands to him, palms upwards, and shrugged questioningly.

"It's fine. She's really cute. She's got two teeth already, and she smiles whenever she sees me." He beamed with pride. There's something so appealing about guys going all gooey about babies, don't you think?

"Aw, bless!"

He went pink again, but with a kind of bashful sheepishness rather than with embarrassment. "She's a honey. What can I say?"

"So what about Lisa?" I braced myself as soon as the words left my mouth, expecting a wisecrack of the "Nope, Lisa's not a honey" variety, but slightly to my surprise none came.

"That's tougher. I guess it depends on how much you want to stay friends with her."

"How d'you mean?"

"Well, it sounds like fairly obsessive behaviour to me. That's a pretty radical crush she's got on this Gabriel guy, and all that eating disorder stuff. She's obviously got issues."

"So what am I supposed to do about it?"

"I don't know. I'm not sure you should do anything. I wouldn't bank on her taking it well if you said something to her about it. She might think you were interfering, or criticizing her or something."

"So what you're saying is, don't say anything to her unless I'm not bothered about us staying friends?"

"Pretty much, yeah." He lifted a shoulder. "I could be wrong, of course. Or you could try telling someone else who might be able to get her some proper help."

"Like who?" I couldn't think of anybody I'd trust with the information.

"Dunno. Old Dobbin, for example. He's supposed to be Head of Pastoral Care, isn't he? Tell him you're concerned about a friend. Let him do some pastoralling for a change, instead of sitting in his office spying on how fast the sixth form are driving their cars into school, or whatever it is he does."

I couldn't imagine going to Mr Dobring about a cut finger, let alone Lisa's issues, but I appreciated Andy's suggestion.

"Thanks, Andy. You're a star. How do you know all this stuff about obsessive behaviour, anyway?"

He gave another shrug. "Psychology. We've been doing it this term." He glanced at his watch. "Shit, is that the time? Better shoot off – I'll catch you later!"

He handed me the books, and I realized he'd been

holding them all the time – had carried them back across the playground for me and everything. What a gent.

It was reassuring to know that Andy understood, but I can't honestly say it made me feel any better about things. At the end of the day this baby was still growing inside my mother (I can't begin to describe just how *bleurgh* it feels to even put that thought into words. . .), and as time passed I kept catching myself just kind of staring at her stomach, transfixed.

"I know," Rupert said to me out of the side of his mouth one day, when Mum had walked past us both on her way to the kitchen – it must have been when he was home for a weekend. "Total gwoss-out, *n'est-ce pas?*"

I think it was the French that did it. Or maybe it was just the fact that she's MY mother and therefore I'm entitled to say or think what I like about her, but criticism from any other source (particularly this one) was another matter entirely.

"What do you mean, 'gross-out'?" I enquired frostily.

He didn't appear to notice the frost. His mistake.

"Her, being in that state. I mean, embawassing or what?" He rolled his eyes theatrically, and I pounced.

"And just how do you think she got in 'that state', you smug little git? Immaculate conception? If your old goat of a father had kept his trousers on. . ."

"Steady on!" he protested. "He's not an old goat! They're *mawwied*, in case you'd forgotten. He is allowed to have—"

"Shut up!" I screeched, and clapped my hands over my ears. "Shut up! Shut up! Shut up!"

Yeah, I know. It was silly, and childish, and unnecessary. All of that. But I knew what he was going to say – "he is allowed to have sex with her" – and I just couldn't bear the thought, either of having the fact shoved down my throat (as it were) *again*, or of hearing Rupert spell it out so graphically. So I decided the best thing was simply to put it out of my mind, shove it far away out of sight, until the baby was born and I'd have no choice but to face it. Which, as it turned out, was my mistake.

Lisa, however, was harder to ignore. I found myself watching her intently at school for any signs of her going off to the Ladies to chuck up after eating. Not that she was doing much eating. Nor, it seemed, much chucking up. None, in fact, or at least not at school. She hardly ever seemed to go to the loo, and when I saw her going I tried to make sure I accompanied her. But nothing. Zilch. Niente. Not so much as a heave.

Her obsession with Gabriel, however, was definitely shifting up a notch or two. Christ knows how it happened – I guess I felt somehow responsible for her, now I knew just what was going on in her head – but I somehow found myself agreeing on a couple of occasions to skulk with her after school in the road outside the vicarage. And a right pranny I felt, too.

"So, um, see anything interesting on telly last night?" I asked her, praying Bex wouldn't see us parading up and down outside like sentries. What on earth would she think? Probably even less of me than she already appeared to do. Just lately she'd begun to make herself scarce whenever Jaz and I were having a natter at school – why would she do that unless she didn't think much of me?

"It's OK." Lisa laughed. "You don't have to make conversation."

"But shouldn't we at least be chatting to each other? What if he sees us?"

"That's the whole point! Why d'you think we're here?" Her laughter tinkled like ice in a tumbler. "Honestly, Mattie. You are funny!"

I personally couldn't think of anything worse than Gabriel glancing out of a window and catching sight of us sauntering past for the umpteenth time. He'd think we'd both lost it. I didn't have a clue what Lisa was hoping to achieve with all this up-and-down-the-roading. So I asked her.

"Achieve?" She pulled a face, like she'd never heard

the word before. "I don't want to *achieve* anything. I just like being near him." She inhaled deeply, a rapt expression on her face, as if she could sense his presence, actually *smell* him. . .

"But how do you know he's even in? He's probably at work."

"He's not. His shift doesn't start until seven this evening."

"So how d'you know *that*?" I already knew, from snooping in her diary, but I just wanted to hear what she'd say.

"I've worked out his shift patterns. I went in just about every day until I figured them out. My cousin used to work there, so I know what the shift hours are." She beamed at me, like a child who'd done something particularly clever. "We ought to do this at night some time. Just imagine – walking past his house when he's fast asleep inside, all tucked up in bed!" And she gave an excited little shiver at the thought.

You know what I should have done at that point? I should have taken her by the elbow and steered her gently away from the pavement outside the vicarage and back to her house, where I should have sat her down and explained to her, in kind, non-accusing terms, that it's not actually considered normal behaviour to patrol the street where somebody lives on the off-chance of catching a glimpse of them, especially not at night; nor to spend so long at their place of work that you can recite the hours they spend there; nor, come to think of it, to make them your sole topic of conversation to the exclusion of everything else. It's not just boring – it's stalking.

But guess what? I didn't. I just didn't have the bottle. I knew Lisa well enough by now to understand that she wasn't going to come quietly. What if she shook me off, refused to listen, screamed the place down? Truth be told, I wasn't altogether sure I'd have come quietly, had our roles been reversed. Nobody likes being told the extent of their crush means they're a nutter, do they? So I allowed her to walk me up and down the road a few more times, and then pleaded a sudden headache plus pressure of homework as a means of escape.

The fact was, this whole thing she had about Gabriel was starting to make me feel really uncomfortable. The *Grease* rehearsals were getting embarrassing, with her constant manoeuvring to stay as close to him as possible. And the sad truth was, he barely seemed to have clocked her existence.

As I think I've mentioned, she and I plus the gaggle of Year Nines had been cast by Lynda Pym as the Pink Ladies. Far less predictably, I'd been given a proper role, with lines to learn and everything. I was Frenchy to Lisa's Rizzo. Luckily for me, as well as the future audience, Frenchy was not only less glamorous but also far less high-profile. If you're familiar with *Grease* you'll know that while Rizzo sashays and struts her way through the entire production in a totally kick-ass way (which Lisa, rather surprisingly, did really well), Frenchy is so far in her shadow as to be practically invisible, her only obvious function being to mastermind the makeover of Sandy from dweeb to vixen with the help of her beauty school training. Or maybe that was just Lynda's take on the characterization.

Being still very much a beginner in the singy-dancey stakes, I was perfectly satisfied with this. I joined in with the Pink Lady choruses on the basis that I could always fall back on my rather brief training in Mrs McLeish's choir and just open and close my mouth at the difficult bits, like a fish, in time with the music. Unfortunately, my plan went majorly pear-shaped when I found out I had to sing a solo.

"A *solo*?" I gasped, feeling suddenly peculiar. I clutched at the back of a chair for support.

"Yes, dear," Lynda said briskly. "'Beauty School Drop-out'. You must know it." And she wiggled her fingers in a commanding way at Gabriel who, sitting at the piano, obligingly started playing. I'd never heard it before in my life. Maybe I'd fallen asleep at that point in the movie.

"Erm. . ." I said, frantically trying to think of a way out of it.

"Don't worry, I'm sure Gabriel will be able to devote a little extra practice time to you."

"I could always sing it instead of Mattie," Lisa piped up hopefully. Fair play to her, she'd managed the solos she'd had to date with considerable aplomb, but Lynda shook her head.

"No, you can't, dear. Rizzo isn't the beauty school dropout, Frenchy is. It's an important point of plotting, don't you see?"

And she drifted off, no doubt to talk to members of the cast who had a firmer grasp of the plotting, leaving me, Lisa, Gabriel and the Year Nines standing around looking at each other.

"I really don't want to do it," I said in an urgent undertone. "I'm crap at singing. Lisa, go and tell her. There must be some way you could do it instead of me. I'm going to balls it up and make a total fool of myself." I could feel the palms of my hands getting all sweaty at just the thought of it.

"No, you won't," Gabriel said kindly. "You'll be fine. It's not even a solo, as such. You sing it with Teen Angel – that's Steve – and a chorus." Steve was about forty and always came to rehearsals in a pinstripe suit and a shirt and tie. Straight from work, obviously. He was a nice chap with a decent voice, not too loud but quite confident. Maybe I'd be all right after all, if I was singing with him. Maybe he'd support me; or better still, drown me out.

"So what do you want me to do? Shall I still go and tell Lynda?" Lisa asked. She dithered around from foot to foot, a slightly disgruntled expression on her face.

"No, Lucy, don't bother. Mattie'll be fine with me." And he gave me a grin.

There was nothing in it but him being friendly and helpful, I swear to God – he was the accompanist, after all – but the look Lisa gave me in return was shot through with pure hatred. Anybody would have thought he'd gone down on one knee and proposed to me. Mind you, I don't suppose him getting her name wrong again helped.

"Actually," she said to him, with what was clearly meant to be a smile, but came out as more of a grimace. "My name's Lisa. Not Lucy. *Lisa*."

But Gabriel was busily tinkling the opening bars of "Beauty School Dropout", and I don't think he even heard her.

Chapter Thirteen

"You may as well admit it – I know you're after him."

I'd only been back in the house for about thirty seconds. I held the phone away from my ear and looked at it, blinking. "Sorry?"

"Don't bother denying it." Lisa's voice at the other end was loud, angry and accusing. "I saw the way you were looking at him. Did you have to be so obvious, coming on to him like that? '*I don't want to do it, I'm crap at singing!*'" she recited in a tantrummy, throwing-a-strop kind of voice that I guessed was supposed to represent me at the rehearsal earlier. She stopped, and there was a moment's silence. "Are you still there?"

I was shocked by her outburst. I didn't know what to say. "I'm still here. I just don't know what you're on about."

"You. And *Gabriel*!" The anger was replaced by a moan of anguish as she said his name. I struggled hard to hold on to my temper. *She's having a tough time,* I told myself. *She doesn't mean it. She can't help it. She's got issues.*

"Lisa," I said in the kind of calm, comforting voice you'd use to reassure a child, or possibly a mad dog that came rushing up barking at you in the street, looking like it was about to take a chunk out of your lower limbs. "You're imagining things. I'm not after him. I don't even fancy him that much any more, now I know he's got a girlfriend. I really can't sing, you of all people should know that by now! He was just being helpful, that's all."

I heard my voice drone on, monotonously, soothingly, along with another voice inside my head that was saying *you're wasting your time, she's not listening to a word,* when she suddenly cut across me.

"Do you really not fancy him any more?"

"Erm. . . Well, no. Not really. I mean, I still think he's hot and everything, but I think Johnny Depp's hot too, and I'm never likely to get off with him either, am I?" I was burbling now. I took a deep breath. "I wasn't cracking on to him, Lisa. Honestly."

"Well. . ." There was another, uncertain pause. "It's just . . . I love him *so much*! I just couldn't bear the thought of. . ." She trailed off, with a sob.

After what felt like another few weeks of this she finally seemed satisfied that I wasn't about to whisk him off on a snogathon – huh, fat chance of that: as if he was interested in *me*! – and after she'd at last hung up I put the phone down, marvelling at how she'd gone from full-on fury, to grief, to resuming her mission to be the future Mrs Foxcroft, all in the space of one phone call. It's not exaggeration to say I was left reeling with majorly mixed emotions. I was relieved that she'd come down from off the ceiling, but baffled by her, too; at a loss to know how to deal with her sudden mood swings. There was definitely something slightly unhinged about her, slightly unstable.

But despite all that, part of me felt a real sympathy for her. I've had my fair share of desperate crushes on lads who were totally unsuitable, or unavailable. Haven't we all? Truth is, I knew that was the moment I should have mentioned the throwing-up thing. It's what a good friend would have done, right? But it had been a long day, what with school and then the *Grease* rehearsal, and then this bonkers phone call. And I still had homework to do. So I bottled out. I didn't say anything.

I still wonder if things might have turned out differently if I had.

A few days later Jaz was, unusually, sitting by herself at lunch. I took my tray and slid into the seat next to her. She looked up and smiled at me.

"Hiya, Mat!"

I was quite taken aback at such a warm greeting. "Bex not with you today?"

A little crease appeared between her eyebrows, the hint of a frown. So much for warmth. "She's off school – got an ear infection. Why d'you ask?"

Because you and she are normally like Siamese twins and nobody else can get a look-in, that's why. . .

I shrugged casually. "No reason. I just wondered."

The frown increased. "We don't come as a matching pair, you know."

"No?"

"No. And even when we are together, it doesn't mean you can't talk to me too."

"OK." I didn't look at her, just forked a mouthful of shepherd's pie into my mouth. At least, that's what the cafeteria said it was. I wasn't even tasting it. It could have been wallpaper paste. I so didn't want to be having this conversation with Jaz. Since when did it become like this between us, uncomfortable and prickly? She was my best mate, for God's sake – my *best mate*.

"But it's not OK." To my surprise and relief, her face softened. She leaned back in her chair slightly, and sighed. "It's not OK, Mat, is it? Why won't you tell me what's wrong?"

"I, erm . . . well . . . it's. . ." I mumbled, pushing the mince and potato round the plate into a glutinous, unappetizing mass. "I just get the feeling Bex doesn't like me very much."

"What?" She frowned again, in a puzzled way. "Why d'you think that?"

"Oh, I don't know. Probably something to do with the way you two are always hanging out together. And the way she makes herself scarce every time I come along."

"Well, the reason we're always together at school is because we're in all the same lessons," she pointed out reasonably.

"So what about out of school?" I could hear the whining tone in my voice. I didn't like it, but I couldn't seem to moderate it. "And why does she do that vanishing act every time she sees me?"

"I didn't realize she did. And I don't see her that much out of school. Not as much as you and I used to see each other, anyway. You're so busy with Lisa these days, you don't seem to have much time for me."

She sounded wistful. I glanced at her; she looked wistful, too. Some kind of emotion welled up in me. I didn't know what it was, but it wasn't unpleasant.

"Aww!" I leaned in towards her and we bumped foreheads affectionately. "I never knew you felt like that! That's what I've been thinking about you and Bex."

"Yeah? Well, there's no need. I mean, I like her and everything, she's awesome, but there's nobody quite like my Mat."

I didn't know what to say. Even if I did I wouldn't have been able to say it, because I suddenly had a big lump in my throat.

"Can I join you guys?" It was Lisa, looming up behind us, carrying a tray with her usual apple-on-a-plate plus glass of water. God knows why she needed a tray. It was hardly a feast.

"Actually," Jaz said, looking up at her and smiling pleasantly, "I don't want to be rude, hon, but would you mind if you didn't? Mat and me are having a bit of a private chat."

The glare Lisa gave her couldn't have been more violent if Jaz had just told her to piss off somewhere else, and to hell with politeness. She took herself off though, nonetheless, flouncing over to an empty table and plonking herself down with much ostentatious scraping of chairs and slamming down of crockery.

"Whoa," Jaz said under her breath. "I wouldn't like to get on the wrong side of her. Did you see the evils she was giving me?"

"Yeah. I'm getting a bit worried about her, to be honest." And I told her, briefly and in an undertone, about Lisa's increasing infatuation with Gabriel, and the whole He'd Love Me If I Was Thin thing. I didn't say how I knew about it, though. How could I tell her I'd been sifting through Lisa's diary?

"D'you think he would?" she mused. "I mean, it

would make him a shallow tosser if he did, but would he look twice at her if she, you know, looked different?"

"Not a chance. There's no – whatever it's called. Spark. Chemistry. She's totally off his radar. He doesn't even know what her name is, he keeps calling her Lucy. Plus he's already got a girlfriend, back in Windsor."

"Ah." Jaz fiddled with her water glass. "No, he hasn't. They've split up. Bex told me. Apparently she sent him a text telling him he was dumped. Nice girl, huh?"

"Oh God!" I was horrified. "Don't tell Lisa that, for Christ's sake! There'll be no stopping her. She'll be hiring a skywriter to put 'Marry Me' up in the sky in vapour trail. . . What?"

Jaz was smirking, her shoulders hunched with the effort of trying not to laugh. "No, nothing. It's just the way you describe it. It's not funny really. It must be difficult for you, trying to cope with her and all that."

"You're not kidding. I feel like a mum with a little kid, having to accompany her to the loo all the time to make sure she's not puking up on the sly."

"Really?" Her eyebrows shot up in surprise. "So she really is doing it, then? She didn't just say she was?"

"Why would she do that?"

"Search me. For effect, for attention?"

"I don't really know whether she is or not, that's the

problem. I haven't actually caught her throwing up, but that doesn't mean she isn't. And all this heavy stuff with Gabriel. . . She even rang me up last night after rehearsal and accused me of trying to cop off with him. I mean, she was really hysterical – like, totally screaming at me down the phone. It's beginning to do my head in."

As I spoke the words I realized the truth of them. It had started out for both of us as just a crush, a bit of harmless fun, but somewhere along the line it had turned into something else entirely for Lisa. Something unhealthy, something desperate. Something dangerous.

"Hmm." Jaz wasn't laughing any more. She looked serious and thoughtful. On the other side of the room, Lisa pushed her chair back with a squeak and stalked from the room without so much as a glance in our direction, breaking St Mark's Cardinal Sin of the Dining Room and leaving her tray and dirty dishes on the table. "She's a strange one, for sure. Remember I told you about how she was with me last year?"

"I remember." I should have taken a bit more notice.

"So what are you going to do?"

"I wish I knew," I replied glumly. "I just wish I knew."

Geoffrey's birthday is on October the thirty-first. I kid you not: it really is on Hallowe'en. Appropriate, or what? I always did think there was something a touch

Gothic about him. Anyway, as I'm sure you know, Hallowe'en always falls in October half-term, and on this particular occasion, Jaz was having a party. Nothing major, she'd said. Just half a dozen mates or so (which in Jaz-speak usually means about twenty). Drinks. Food. Silly kiddy games like apple-bobbing and face-painting and telling each other ghost stories – that kind of stuff. Oh, and I thought we'd have fancy-dress, she told me. I've got the *fabbest* Catwoman outfit. . . It sounded like super-cool fun, and just the sort of thing I needed as a break from all the heavy Lisa and Mum-being-preggers stuff that had been going on.

Well. Guess what? Mum wouldn't let me go. Well, OK. Maybe that's putting it a tad strongly, I mean she didn't actually forbid me on pain of death. She just went into disappointed mode, which is her normal ploy for getting me to see things her way. It's a killer – the big sad eyes, the down-turned mouth, the sorrowful expression. The implication that it's entirely up to me, of course, but if I do decide to carry on regardless she's likely to go into an emotional decline that she's unlikely to recover from, and I wouldn't want the guilt of *that* on my conscience, now would I. . .?

This is how it went.

Mum: But it's Geoffrey's birthday.

Mattie (simultaneously lifting left shoulder, eyebrow

and side of lip): And. . .?

Mum: And I'm making a special supper.

Mattie: Well, you won't want me playing gooseberry then, will you?

Mum: It's a special *family* supper. Of course we want you there, darling. (*Wheedlingly, like I'm five years old.*) There's even going to be a cake!

Mattie: Mum. Let me explain. Jaz is having a Hallowe'en party that night. I've hardly seen anything of her lately. . . (yadda yadda yadda)

Mum: Oh, well, if you'd prefer to spend a special family occasion with your friends. . . (Cue terminal disappointment, guilt trip a-go-go, and crumbling of Mattie's defences. The End.)

Only it wasn't the end, of course, because I then had to tell Jaz I wasn't going to be able to go to her Hallowe'en do after all, and she immediately jumped to the conclusion that it was because I was going to be doing something with Lisa instead. She was fine about it once we'd got the misunderstanding cleared up, but let's just say that, what with one thing and another, I wasn't exactly looking forward to Geoffrey's birthday tea.

But even after that unpromising beginning, it still didn't start off too badly. Better than I'd been expecting, at any rate. Mum had taken Geoffrey out for the day, having spent the entire previous evening preparing a proper feast. True, it was a relentlessly veggie feast, but a feast nonetheless: quiches and pasties, bowls of couscous and guacamole and hummus, four different types of salad and three different types of bread – it all looked great. It smelled even better. My stomach rumbled as I stood looking at it, and even Rupert managed to summon up some enthusiasm.

"Yum, yum," he said. "That looks nice. What are they?" He pointed to the pasties.

"Those are feta and kidney bean, and those are tofu and mushroom," Mum replied.

His smile faltered a little at that, but fair play to him, he still managed to hang on to it.

"Gosh. How – umm – unusual."

As for the birthday boy himself, I think it's fair to say he was made up.

"Oh wow," he kept exclaiming. "Look at this wonderful spread! Wow! And you did it all without me knowing anything about it! Nobody's cooked for me for my birthday for years! It's – wow!"

It was as if he'd invented the word. It was actually quite funny. He just so isn't the type of person from whose lips the word "wow" falls naturally. Moll and I exchanged glances, and she had to bite on her lower lip and turn her head away to stop herself from laughing.

Anyway, we all sat down and began to tuck in, and

Mum opened the bottle of nearly-champagne with a great deal of ceremony and panache, if rather a lot of spillage; when she brought the cake in we all sang "Happy Birthday" and then applauded, and Geoffrey cut it after obediently blowing out the candles, and even made a little speech about how lovely it was to spend a birthday being spoilt by the people he cared most about in the world. He looked round the table at all of us as he said it, and went rather dewy-eyed. It was hard not to, dammit. Even *I* felt a prickle behind my eyes, and had to swallow. It was all going terribly well – until the phone went.

"I'll get it," I said, jumping to my feet. I was semi-expecting it to be Jaz, who said she'd ring later, if Surjit felt like coming over to pick me up, to see if I'd done my stepdaughterly duty and Mum would let me go over for an hour or so. But it wasn't Jaz. When I picked up the phone, there was nothing but silence. I kept saying "hello", just in case there was a dodgy connection or something, but still nothing. After a few moments of this the dialling tone cut in: whoever it was had obviously hung up. I rang 1471, but was told the caller had withheld their number, so was none the wiser. I hate it when that happens. Call me paranoid – and I guess I was feeling rather more sensitive about these things than normal because of all the Lisa stuff – but I always imagine it's some kind of stalker.

Puzzled, I went back into the kitchen, where the others were still sitting around the table. What was left of the birthday tea had been pushed to the end of it and all the dirty plates piled up, out of the way, and they were all looking at some papers that were spread all around.

"Who was it?" Molly asked me.

"Nobody."

"Wrong number?" Mum asked, glancing up from the paper she was looking at. She pushed it across the table to Moll. "Here, what do you think of this one?"

"Not a wrong number – nobody. There was nobody there, the line was just dead. What's all that stuff?"

I walked across and picked one up. It was an estate agent's details of a house, a single sheet of A4-sized paper with a picture at the top, and below it a printed description. I started to read it: *Lovely family home set in beautiful open Devon countryside, this stunning barn conversion has been lovingly renovated and restored by the present owners and boasts a multitude of...*

"Mmm. Nice house. But why have you got this?" I waved the paper. Nobody answered me. I took a step closer. All the papers on the table were the same thing: details of different houses. There must have been more than thirty of them.

"Why are you looking at all this stuff?" I asked, in a louder voice. "House descriptions?"

"Oh, dur," Molly said, hitting her forehead in an elaborate manner with the heel of her hand. "Because we're moving?"

There was a horrible silence, then everybody started talking at once.

"Darling, please don't think. . ." said Mum.

"It's not that we. . ." said Geoffrey.

"It's no big. . ." said Molly.

"It's because of. . ." said Rupert.

He was sitting closest to me, so he was the one I turned to.

"Because of what? No, go on, tell me. I'm interested."

"Well – because of the baby, I suppose." He shot a glance across the table to his father. It was a kind of She's a Loony, Get Me Out of Here glance, and it made me so mad.

"Because of the *baby*? Oh, right. So what you're saying is that this baby is so important that it can't be expected to live here, it's got to live in a poncy *barn conversion* costing –" I looked down at the details again. "– costing *half a million quid*? Bloody hell! How the hell are you going to afford that?" I looked at Mum. "Seriously, unless Geoffrey's been chosen to be the next presenter of *Time Team*, how are you going to find that kind of money?"

"Mattie," Mum murmured with a pained expression. "Please. . ." She got up and started clearing the dishes away, as a way of shutting me up, fending me off. It was obvious why she was doing it.

"Well, just tell me then. I'm interested," I repeated, even though I wasn't interested, I was furious. Furious that everybody appeared to know about this decision to move house, to move away from where Mum and Moll and I had been living perfectly happily since leaving behind our past life, of Manchester, and Dad, and all that this implied. Furious that everybody seemed to think that this teensy-weensy little cottage had been perfectly fine up till now, but now this baby was on the way, we suddenly had to move to some great big *mansion*. . . Everybody, that is, apart from me. And Mum apparently didn't even see the need to talk to me about it.

"God, Mat, chill! What's the big deal? And it's not necessarily going to be there," Molly told me, holding out a handful of the wretched papers towards me. "There's loads of places it might be – look. There's some well cool houses here."

I couldn't believe she didn't *know* what the big deal was. "You needn't sound so happy about it." I glared at her, refusing to take them. "This is our home – why do we have to move at all?" *And why am I the last to find out about it?*

"Erm – if I could just. . ." Geoffrey began apologetically. He cleared his throat. "If I could just explain? I can see why you're upset, but it was unfortunate timing. It must have looked as if Rupert and Molly knew all about it and you didn't, but really, Alice and I had only just dug the estate agents' blurbs out, while you were answering the phone. We should have waited until you were back in the room, though. I realize that now. I really am sorry, Mattie."

I hesitated, torn. How could I shove his apology back in his face? It was the guy's birthday, when all was said and done. On the other hand, I still couldn't see the need to move house. Or why everybody else was acting as if it was already a done deal, and to hell with what I thought about it.

"I don't see why we've got to move house at all," I muttered sullenly.

Molly sighed, mock-patiently. "Because of the baby. Like Rupes said. There's hardly room for the five of us in this titchy little cottage. How d'you think we're going to squeeze a baby in as well?"

I stared at her, infuriated beyond speech. It was the "Rupes" that did it. Since when did my sister start calling him by his father's pet-name? It made me feel as if she was siding with him against me.

Then Rupert compounded her sin by opening his own mouth.

"Don't you think," he said to me mildly, "that we should be pulling together and supporting our parents on this, wather than getting all cwoss with them?"

"Support them?" I said, so incensed I could barely force the words out. "Like you were supporting them when you said my mother being pregnant was a total gross-out? Is that what you mean by support?"

He turned red and started stuttering and mumbling, but I didn't care. To tell the truth, it barely registered. I couldn't bear being in the same room as him; as any of them. How dared they leave me out of important family decisions? I turned on my heel and stalked out, before I could do what I really wanted to do and pick up all the house details and chuck them – childishly, histrionically – all over the kitchen floor.

Extract from my diary:

Why is my life so shit? Would anybody care if I disappeared? Or died? Would they even notice?

Chapter Fourteen

I could have killed Mum for not letting me go to Jaz's Hallowe'en do. It had been such a long time since Jaz and I had done anything together without Lisa hanging around in the background. There just seemed to have been so many misunderstandings between us since Lisa had been on the scene – there was no way, for example, that a few months ago, Jaz would have thought "it's my stepfather's birthday tea" actually meant "I'm hanging out with Lisa". Or anybody else, for that matter. She used to take what I said at face value; now, it was as if, in her eyes, I'd handed her Best Mate status over to Lisa.

It began to dawn on me that many of the things that were bugging me were connected with Lisa in some way (apart from the obvious, I mean). I was pretty sure Jaz wouldn't have become quite so pally quite so soon with Bex had I not been monopolized by Lisa during the summer holidays while Jaz was away in France. If we hadn't drifted apart, I'd have been able to tell her about Mum being pregnant, and confide in her my concerns about Molly – I still didn't know what was up with her, but a couple of times she'd got on the school bus home with her eyes definitely pink and watery-looking, and I'd woken up once to hear her in her bed across the other side of the room, sobbing quietly to herself in the dark. Concerned, I'd called her name, but she'd stopped immediately, and when I turned on my bedside light she was lying on her side facing away from me, still as a corpse, pretending to be asleep.

If Lisa hadn't come between Jaz and me I'd have told her about Molly ages ago, told her I was at a loss to know what to do about my sister who was normally so perky and smiley and sensible, and asked for her advice, or at least her opinion. It was no use talking to Molly herself about it. She'd already made it plain it wasn't up for discussion.

But somehow, I just didn't feel I could suddenly pick things up with Jaz as though nothing had changed between us. And I certainly didn't feel I could tell her any more about Lisa and her increasingly weird behaviour, as it seemed important to convince Jaz that *she* was still the most important friend in my life, not Lisa. And how was I going to do that, if the first thing I talked to her about was – well, Lisa?

Apart from anything else, it wasn't as easy as just dropping the one friend in favour of the other. I'd managed to fend Lisa off quite a bit over half-term by using loads of homework and "family stuff" as an excuse not to invite her round, and had tried to continue the weening-off process once we were all back at school. But like I say, it wasn't that easy. For a start, Jaz and Bex were still almost always hanging out together in school, so it was hard to catch Jaz by herself. Added to which, despite what Jaz had said, Bex definitely seemed to have a problem with me. Every time they were together and I went over to talk to them Bex would smile politely, and nod, and even manage to contribute a comment or two, before coming up with some excuse to detach herself from us and walk away, with that easy swinging lope that reminded me so much of the way Gabriel moved.

One time, though, it didn't happen like that.

One lunch time when I walked into the sixth-form block, there was a group of people sitting over by the window with Jaz and Bex at the centre. Or rather, with Bex at the centre. Jaz was sitting on a beanbag on the edge, and looked up when I came in. She smiled, and put up an arm and waved at me, a kind of beckoning flourish to summon me over. But just as I started to move in her direction there was a familiar voice in my ear.

"Hi Mattie," it said breathlessly. "Have you learnt those lines for *Grease* yet? Only I was just wondering if—"

"Sorry." I pinned a smile on my face and turned to face her. "I was just going over to have a word with Jaz."

Lisa looked over the group by the window. There were half a dozen or so: Jaz, and a girl called Hollie from our year; Andy, and his mate Seb Rollins, and a couple of others from the Upper Sixth; and in the middle, holding centre stage in typically animated fashion, Bex.

"Cool," Lisa said, eagerly. "I'll come over too. You don't mind, do you?"

It was a statement, not a question. We went over and joined them, pulling up a beanbag each. There was only room next to Jaz for me, so Lisa ended up opposite me, next to Seb. It soon became apparent that he and Bex were involved in a heated debate about something, with the others acting more as onlookers or, in one or two cases, egging-onners.

"I still reckon it takes bottle," Seb was saying, "to do it in front of a bunch of strangers."

Bex shrugged. "Bottle, shmottle. You just have to not care what people think of you."

I whispered in Jaz's ear, "What's this all about?"

"Life class." She saw my blank expression. "You know – taking your clothes off for art students so they can draw you?"

I remembered that Seb was good at art, very good in

209

fact; he was tipped for a place at one of the big art schools in London after A levels.

"Bet you wouldn't do it, though," Andy put to Bex, with a grin.

"I wouldn't," Hollie said, fanning her face with a hand like a scandalized Jane Austen matron. "The thought of all those horny students having a good gawp! No thanks."

"Bloody nerve! We're not horny, we have to study the unclothed body so we can make our representations of it anatomically correct," Seb protested, but Andy was having none of it.

"You mean like wotsisname – Picasso? Three eyes and a nose coming out of your cheek – that kind of anatomically correct? Yah, you're all talk, you arty-farty types!"

"I'd do it. In fact, I've done it." Bex spoke quietly, but everybody shut up nonetheless.

"You've *done it*?" said Seb, asking the question we were all thinking. "How d'you mean?"

"I mean, I've posed naked. Not for a life class, though. For a friend's A level art project. At my last school."

There was a moment's shocked silence, which was broken by Andy.

"When you say *naked*. . ." he began.

Bex looked at him, square on. "I mean naked."

"What – totally?"

"Mm-hmm. As the day I was born."

Andy gave her a long appraising look, then licked his lips thoughtfully. "Straight up? Well, bugger me." I knew exactly what was going through his mind. So, I'm sure, did everybody else.

"I've got A level coursework," Seb said, looking pensive. "I haven't decided what to do yet. I don't suppose you'd. . .?"

"Don't mind." Bex shrugged casually. "If you want me to. It'll cost you though."

"Cost me? How d'you mean?"

"You don't think those life-class models turn up and get their kit off out of the kindness of their hearts, do you? They get paid a fee. Mine's fifty quid," she said, examining her fingernails nonchalantly. Everybody laughed, including Seb, knowing he'd been had.

"Ha! She's got you there, mate! What d'you reckon the chances are of him actually coming up with the dosh, just to prove art students aren't horny?" Andy asked Bex.

She laughed, throwing her head back, enjoying the joke. "Slim to anorexic, I'd say."

It was a chance remark. She didn't mean anything by it – she couldn't have. Everybody else was still laughing, and probably didn't even hear it. But I heard, and so, I knew, had Lisa. Sitting opposite her, I saw the look that passed over her face. She got up from her beanbag, clumsily, her hair swinging forward to hide her expression, but just then the bell went for lessons and everybody else started getting up too, still chatting and laughing about Bex and Seb's exchange.

"That was class," Jaz said to Bex, smiling. "I must get my stuff for English. I'll see you guys there, yeah?"

"Yup," I said distractedly. I was trying to spot Lisa through the others, wondering about the anorexic remark, whether it had been the cue for her to go off to the Ladies for a quick chuck-up. A twinge of annoyance passed through me. Why did I feel so responsible for her, yet unable to offer her any proper help? I didn't even feel I could talk to Lisa herself about it, was afraid of the confrontation, of possibly setting her off into bonkers mode again.

I caught Bex's eye. "Are you coming to English, then?" she asked me with a friendly smile.

It was the smile that did it. *Oh, stuff it. Let Lisa look after herself for once. . .* "Yeah, sure. Listen Bex, can I ask you something?"

"Course you can."

"I was just wondering whether you . . . well, whether there's a problem. It's just, every time I go to talk to Jaz and you're there you seem to. . . It just seems as if you don't. . ." I floundered, and then trailed off, hopelessly.

"You think I don't like you – is that it?"

It took the wind out of my sails a bit, I have to admit, but you know what? I admired her for having the guts to just say it without beating around the bush, like I'd done. Her directness and openness was what I'd liked about her in the beginning, I remembered. When we'd first met. It seemed like such a long time ago now.

It seemed best to respond by being equally to-the-point. "OK then. So tell me – do you like me?"

She shrugged. "Sure I like you. It's your obsession with my brother I'm not so keen on."

"Obsession with your. . .?" The penny dropped. "Oh no, no! That's not me, that's Lisa. I mean, I did like him – I still do, I think he's great – just not in that way any more. But Lisa – whoa, what can I say? She's, like, besotted!"

Damn it, why did I have to spoil it by wittering? But Bex didn't seem to notice. "Yeah, Jaz told me."

"But you don't believe her?"

"I do now you've explained." She looked at me and smiled, and it was as if the sun had suddenly come out. Everything just felt so much brighter and lighter. "I believe you, Mattie. It's not a problem any more."

"But . . . why was it such a problem when you thought I did? Like your brother, I mean."

"I haven't got a problem with people liking him."

She lifted a shoulder. "How weird would that make me? Liking's fine, it's all that *oh Gabriel, you're so gorgeous, oh Gabriel, I'm in love with you* crap that does my head in. You know what? Since I was twelve, girls have wanted to be mates with me only so they can have a crack at my brother."

I nodded sympathetically. "That must be hard."

"It's made knowing who wants to be friends with me for *me* pretty hard. That's what I thought about you, that once you'd caught sight of Gabriel, you only wanted. . ." She tailed off, and I felt guilty as hell. After all, I could hardly put my hand on my heart and say that had never occurred to me, could I? But again, Bex didn't seem to notice.

"Can I tell you something?" she asked suddenly.

"Of course you can!" Anything to get off ulterior motives for wanting to be her mate. "What is it?"

She cocked her head to one side. It was if she was assessing me, my trustworthiness. "The reason we moved up here. Away from Windsor. If I tell you, you mustn't tell anybody else."

I suddenly remembered Molly, ages ago, telling me abut the Chinese Whispers. The gossip she'd heard, that the Foxcrofts had been forced to move by some deep, dark secret. "I won't tell anybody else. Don't worry. What is it?"

"My mother had an affair. With a parishioner. It was

just too much for my dad to have to stay in his old church, with all the gossip, so he asked the bishop for a move." She looked me straight in the eye as she said it, her gaze clear and direct, her voice quiet, matter-of-fact. But I could tell she felt anything but matter-of-fact about it.

"Oh God!" I was genuinely horrified. "How awful for you!"

She glanced down. "Thanks. Thanks for not laughing."

"Why on earth would I laugh? I don't see anything funny in it."

"You'd be amazed what people find to laugh about when it involves vicars. Some of the kids at my old school though it was the funniest thing they'd heard in their lives. My mum left my dad, in case you're wondering. It wasn't enough for her just to have an affair, she moved in with her . . . moved in with him. Gabe and I haven't seen her since."

It made my family troubles – my mother, happily married to a man she loved, pregnant with his child – seem trifling and run-of-the-mill by comparison.

"I'm really sorry," I said again. What else could I say?

"Thanks. I just thought I'd tell you because it might explain why I've been a bit – you know. Odd."

"You haven't been odd. I think you're great." I put an

arm round her shoulders. Suddenly, all my vague jumbled worries, about her having stolen Jaz away from me, about Jaz preferring her to me, had disappeared.

She hugged me back. "Thanks, Mattie. I think you're great, too."

In English, Jaz told me that Hollie had told *her* that Lisa had gone home. She hadn't been feeling too good after lunch, apparently, and had left school. I should have been concerned about her, I know. I should have rung her to see how she was, but all I could think of in English was how great it was to be free of her for once. Jaz and I sat next to each other, just like old times; Bex sat just in front, with Hollie, and there was this little note thing going on between the three of them, about how Andy fancied me. It was all really light-hearted and pretty childish, but it cheered me up no end to a) revert back to girly ooh-he-fancies-you stuff in a fun way after the whole Lisa/Gabriel thing, and b) to be in the centre of it, for a change. Even though c) it also featured Andy, and d) we all knew there was nothing in it.

My light-heartedness came to a pretty abrupt end, though. Around half nine that evening I was upstairs doing homework when Mum poked her head round the bedroom door.

"Telephone for you," she said. "One of your friends. She seems a bit upset."

It was Lisa. Sobbing so hard I couldn't make out what she was saying.

"What?" I kept repeating. "What? Lisa, what is it? What's the matter?" My heart was thumping up in my throat, my hands clammy with panic. What if she'd done something stupid?

Eventually, I managed to grasp something of what she was saying.

"Mattie, it's awful. Come round. Please."

"Stay there." I tried to inject as much calmness and authority into my voice as I could muster. "Don't do anything. I'll be with you as soon as I can."

As I hung up I became aware of Geoffrey, standing in the sitting room doorway.

"Is everything all right?"

"Yes . . . no . . . I don't know! It's one of my friends, she's, I just think something might have. . ." I stood there and put my hands up to my face, trying to focus my wildly jumping thoughts. "Geoffrey, I know it's getting late, and I know it's a bit of a cheek, but could you possibly—"

"I'll drive you there," he cut across me. "Of course I will. You get your coat on. I'll go and back the car out."

The Volvo was waiting out on the lane for me, and Geoffrey drove to Combe Bridge in record time. Not that it felt fast: the time dragged and the journey was in slo-mo while my brain rapidly filled with thoughts of what Lisa might have done to herself, images of what I might find when I got there, each scarier and more gory than the last.

As we drew up outside Lisa's house Geoffrey said to me, "Would you like me to come in with you?"

"No, no," I assured him, in a voice that was about a hundred times more confident than I felt. "It'll be fine. I'm sure it'll be fine. She can be a bit – you know. Melodramatic."

"Well, if you're sure. I'll be waiting out here for you."

"No need. It'll be fine. I'll make my own way home."

He didn't argue. I didn't know whether I felt relieved or dismayed. A mixture of both, probably. As I got out of the car he pressed something into my hand. I looked down at it, in the dim orange sodium glow cast by the street light above us. It was a ten-pound note.

"Get a cab back," he told me. "Call home when you're ready and I'll order one for you."

I was touched. "Aw, thanks. There's no need, I can easily go to the bus station and—"

"There's every need. And Mattie – if you need me to come back, for any reason, just ring. Promise?"

Our eyes met. "I promise."

I walked up the path with trepidation, and rang the bell. The door opened almost immediately, as if Lisa had been standing there waiting for me to arrive. Perhaps she had been. She was wearing pyjamas, pink brushed cotton with a white heart design, and a pink fleece dressing gown. A large tabby cat was cradled in her arms, purring throatily, its amber eyes half-closed with pleasure.

"I've been so silly," Lisa said, with a little giggle. "I thought it was a burglar, and it was Tibby all the time. He must have got in through the utility room window."

Relief flooded through me. Relief, and a strong, almost overwhelming desire to take her by her shoulders and shake her.

"You mean," I said, through gritted teeth, "you got me to come all the way over here at this time of night because of a *cat*?"

"It's not my cat," she said hastily, as if that made everything all right. "It's next door's. He's always finding his way in. He knows his Auntie Lisa gives him nice foodies, don't 'oo? Don't 'oo, precious?" She lowered her face to his and he, the big girl's blouse, rubbed his nose ecstatically around hers. He was drooling with bliss. She looked up at me again. "It's not that late, is it?"

Irritation sliced through me. I fought it down, with an effort. I'm not normally a violent person, but I really wanted to slap her. "It's gone ten o'clock. I was in the middle of an English essay. I thought you were in major trouble. My stepfather drove me over, he offered to come in with me to make sure you were OK."

"Aw, that was nice of him!" She looked at me more closely, and her mouth drooped at the corners. "You're cross with me. I can tell."

"No shit, Sherlock!" I gave up on trying to maintain control. "Have you any idea what was going through my mind? What kind of thing I was imagining?"

"I know. I mean, yes, I can imagine." Suddenly grave, she put the cat down through the still-open front door, ushered me in, and closed it behind me. "Please don't be cross with me. I'm sorry. But I heard all these noises downstairs, and I tried to tell myself it was nothing, but I was all by myself, and—"

"What d'you mean, all by yourself?" I interrupted. "Where're your parents?"

"Dad's in Dubai, I think, and Mum's gone to see a friend. She's staying overnight, she said her friend's going through a messy divorce and she needs wine and sympathy. It's all right, Mattie. I am seventeen, after all!"

She didn't look it, standing there barefoot in her PJ's, her eyes wide with wounded innocence. She looked more Molly's age – younger. Far too little and vulnerable to be left by herself overnight. Far too dizzy and panicky, too. It was impossible to stay annoyed with her; it would have been like whipping a puppy.

I sighed. "It's OK. It doesn't matter."

I followed her into the kitchen. She opened the fridge and took out a bottle of Diet Coke, splashed some into two glasses, and handed me one.

"Want anything to eat?"

I told her I was fine, but she rooted round in a cupboard nonetheless, and brought out a family-sized pack of kettle crisps and one of tortilla chips. She tore both of them open and began to cram them in her mouth by the handful, as though she was starving.

"Blimey, Lisa," I said jokily. "Didn't you have any tea?"

"Actually, no, I didn't," she said, through the bits of crisp. "I didn't have any lunch, either."

There was a moment's silence, broken only by her munching. *To hell with it*, I thought. *In for a penny. . .*

"Have you been making yourself throw up?" I said. My voice seemed to echo around the vast kitchen. *Throw up, throw up, up, up. . .* She looked at me guiltily, crumbs of Doritos adhering to the corners of her mouth.

"No-o," she said. Her voice rose at the end of the word, like a challenge. *So what are you going to do about it?*

I persisted. "Are you sure?"

She seemed to crumple then, to kind of fold up, get smaller. "I did try," she confessed. "Once or twice. It was horrible, though. I've always hated being sick."

"But . . . why? Why did you even try?"

"Because I'm so *fat*," she wailed. She pulled up her pyjama top, grabbed a teeny piece of non-existent flab from her waist. "Look at me! I've got to lose weight somehow."

"Lisa." I put down my glass of Coke and went over to her. Put my hands on her shoulders. Somehow stopped myself from giving her a slap. "Look at me. You are not fat. For God's sake, how many times! You. Are. Not. *Fat!*"

"OK, OK already!" She laughed, falsely, and squirmed her way from my grasp. "I believe you! I've actually lost nearly a stone in under a month, so I'm feeling pretty pleased with myself."

It seemed a lot to me, but what do I know? I've never tried to diet in my life. I enjoy my food too much. "How did you manage that?"

"Just by cutting down. It's amazing what junk you eat without even realizing." Her eyes glowed with a kind of religious fervour. "I feel so different now I'm beginning to get rid of it. People who are naturally slim don't understand what it's like for fatties like me. People like Jaz and Bex. It's all right for them."

I ignored the "fatties like me" comment. "So what did you make of what Bex said at school earlier?"

"Pfft. Does she think we're gullible, or what?" she said, with scorn. "All that rubbish about posing in the nude for her friend's art project!"

It was such a Lisa-like way of putting it. *In the nude*. Everybody else I knew would have said naked, starkers, with her kit off. In any case, I'd meant Bex's "slim to anorexic" throwaway comment, not her claim to bare-assed fame.

"So what did you think about it?" I asked her carefully.

"Well, she was obviously lying," she declared. "As if she'd do that kind of thing! I'd certainly never do it – not if you paid me a million pounds, never mind fifty!"

It didn't seem to occur to her that perhaps Bex was different to her, more confident about herself, her body.

"Maybe," I started, but she had grown bored with talking about Bex.

"Look," she said. "I want to show you something. But it's really, like, private?"

Oh God, I groaned, in my head. *Not more secrets! Please, not more secrets. . .*

She bent down behind the counter, and re-emerged with a blue plastic folder. "I know it needs some more work doing on it, but I'd really value your opinion."

She handed the folder to me. I looked at it, at arm's length. "What is it?"

Lisa put her head on one side, coyly. "Just – something I've been doing."

"Not something to do with Gabriel, by any chance?"

"I'm not saying anything about it. You'll have to read

it." She picked up her glass of Coke, took a long swig. "I'm going to get him, you know. I love him. He's not going to stand a chance, not when he realizes just how determined I am to make him love me back."

"Lisa." I didn't know what to say, what I *could* say that she would take any notice of. I'd said it all before. "He's his own person. He's got his own thoughts and feelings. You can't make him love you."

She set her mouth, stubbornly. "Yes, I can."

"No, you can't! He's going away after Christmas, remember? He's going to be a ski instructor in France."

"Then I'll stop him going. He's got to realize," she whispered, "he's *got to*."

"But you can't stop him going!"

She looked at me then. Stared straight into my eyes. There was something strange burning at the back of hers, something hot and obsessive.

"Yes, I can," she whispered. "I can stop him. And I'm going to. I am going to, Mattie. Trust me."

And that's when I realized she'd finally lost the plot.

Chapter Fifteen

His name was Gabriel, which is pretty appropriate given that the first time I saw him I thought he was an angel. The sun was behind him, glinting through his hair, and he looked like he had a halo. He smiled at me and said hello, and I knew from that moment on that we were destined to be together. I had met my soulmate. My heart was his for ever.

A lot has happened since then. Time has moved on and healed the wounds, the many wounds. Dried the tears I cried over him, so many tears, oceans of tears. The bitter pain and the anguish of having him almost snatched from under my very nose has faded. He never said he loved me but he knew I loved him, he tried to stop me but my heart had decided. There was nothing I could do about it. There was nothing he could do about it. There was nothing either of us could do about it. It was destined to be.

His name was Gabriel, and the very first time I saw him I was in love. It was as simple as that. As simple as that, and as complicated as that. Both simple and complicated...

It was at this point that I began to lose the will to live. I glanced down at the loose papers inside the blue folder. There were dozens of them, all covered with the same close typescript. I didn't even know what the thing was meant to be – a story, a journal, random jottings, an account of her enthralling non-existent love affair? *Jesus...* I pulled out another page, at random, and began to read it.

...into his arms and covered my neck with dozens of kisses. My gasp of pleasure filled the room, and he took this as encouragement to continue. He undid the zip at the back of my dress and ran his hands across my back, slowly, and then put them inside and moved them round so that he was touching my—

GOD! It was virtually pornographic! The dreadfulness of it had a kind of compulsive fascination, though. I read some more. It was full of Gabriel's "throbbing manhood" and "thrusting need", and Lisa (in her literary parallel-universe) doing a lot of sobbing and thrashing around while being groped a fair bit. A snort of laughter escaped down my nose. I couldn't help it, the whole thing was just so . . . *awful.*

It reminded me of the story Rupert had written, back in the bad old days when Moll and I used to torment him by calling him Tin Grin. I'd discovered it on his computer when I'd been snooping around in his room (OK, I know; I'm not proud of it), featuring him in the guise of the Mighty Warrior Ty'n Grhyn, with me as the Bitch Queen M'Atil Daa, and Molly as . . . actually I can't remember what he'd cast Moll as, but I'm sure you get the picture. On the face of it, his story and Lisa's whatever-it-was bore little or no resemblance to each other, but they were similar in that they were both a) total fantasy, and b) utter crap.

Still snorting, I put the pages carefully back inside the blue folder. I'd give it back to her at school tomorrow. Then I remembered. She'd asked me for my opinion; what on earth could I say to her when she asked me what I'd thought of it? That wiped the smirk off my face, I can tell you. On second thoughts, perhaps I ought to hang on to it for a bit longer.

When I turned up at the church hall that week for *Grease*, I had a bit of surprise. No, scrub that – I had a big shock. For there, standing chatting to the usual reception committee of Mavis-the-walnut-woman and Percy, her sidekick, was none other than Andy. I couldn't imagine why he was there.

"Hello!" I exclaimed, going over. "What on earth are you doing here?"

"Do you know this young man?" Mavis beamed up at him, her brown face creasing into a thousand wrinkles.

"He was just telling us how much he enjoys all the old-fashioned, singy-dancey stuff," Percy put in.

"You do?" I turned to Andy. "Wow. I never knew that!"

Andy was starting to look decidedly pink about the ears. "Well . . . I'd heard about you guys and all the fun and games that goes on up here of a Wednesday evening, so I thought I'd – y'know. Give it a go!" He waggled his hands in front of his face, fingers spread, palms outward. Laughing, Mavis and Percy copied the gesture.

"It's *Showtime*!" Percy said, snuffling with amusement.

"Well, well, well!" Lisa had appeared behind me, making me jump. "Look who it isn't!"

"You know this young lady as well?" Mavis exclaimed. She sounded delighted. "I can't tell you how wonderful it is to have all this young blood on board. Lynda is going to be *so* thrilled!"

"Who's Lynda?" Andy asked me.

"The producer. Do you really like all the old-fashioned, singy-dancey stuff?" I was fascinated by the thought. Somehow, I'd never seen Andy as a fan of musicals. I'd always had him down more as a Bruce Willis, Vin Diesel, Marilyn Manson kind of boy.

"Sure," he said, shrugging. "Why not? I'll give it a go. I sing a bit, play guitar; you know. . ."

"*Do* you?" I'd never known that either. "How about dancing? You any good at that? There's a lot of dancing in *Grease*."

Lisa laughed merrily, and tucked her arm companionably through Mavis's. "You know what? I reckon I know the real reason Andy's here." She gave her a big, cheesy wink, and Mavis, the daft bat, fell right into the trap.

"What's that then, dear?"

"Mattie."

"What – you mean. . .?" Mavis looked at each of us in turn, the penny dropping. (At that moment I wanted it to drop right on Lisa's head, preferably along with about a thousand more of its little brothers and sisters. Pennies from heaven. That would've shut her up.) "You mean . . . *romance*?" Mavis whispered the word coyly, and Lisa smirked.

"Mm-hm. You know – *Andy and Mattie up a tree, K-I-S-S-I-N-G!*" she recited, in an irritating sing-song tone.

For the second time in less than a week, I could have smacked her one. And judging by Andy's face, it was a feeling he shared.

Mortified, I looked down at the floor; felt the blood rushing to my face, couldn't look at Andy, couldn't look at anyone. Which was odd, considering what Lisa had said wasn't even true.

"Wow, Lisa," Andy was remarking drily. "That's the first time I've heard anybody come out with that outside the playground since I was in the Juniors."

Lisa just simpered and took herself over to her usual post by the piano, and Mavis and Percy drifted off to chat to Lynda. Which left me and Andy standing by ourselves.

"Sorry about her," I muttered to him, still looking at the floor. "I don't know where on earth she got the idea that—"

"Don't worry about it," he cut across me abruptly. "She was only stirring. Is that lover boy, then? Bex's bro?" He nodded over to Gabriel, who was listening distractedly to Lisa in full flow, hands waving around as if she was conducting an orchestra. I wondered what she was talking about. Proposing they eloped together, maybe. Or debating what names they should call their children.

"It's Gabriel, yeah. He's a bloody good pianist, actually." I don't know why I felt the need to say that, like I had to stick up for him or something. Andy was going to discover for himself pretty soon just how good a pianist Gabriel was.

"Hmph." Andy didn't sound impressed. "He looks a bit of a ponce to me."

At that moment Lynda came sailing over to us, all flowing garments and big burgundy hair.

"Lynda Pym," she said to Andy, sticking out a hand and flashing her large tombstone-like teeth at him. "Producer of this shebang. Sweetie, Mavis tells me you can sing. Is it true? You can help us out of a frightful hole if it is. Our Teen Angel has had to bow out – how would you feel about stepping into his shoes?"

She bore him away, and I went dispiritedly over to the piano where Lisa was still holding forth to Gabriel, surrounded by the other Pink Ladies (aka Starey, Drooly, Giggly et al) who were standing around inelegantly, chewing gum and looking bored rigid.

"Gabriel," I said, looking demurely up at him from under my eyelashes. "Could you be total babe and run through 'Beauty School Dropout' with me one more time while Lynda's still busy over there? I'm still not sure I've got that middle bit right."

It was a bit of a cheap trick, but I knew he wouldn't cotton on that I was only doing it to get back at Lisa for her "Andy fancies Mattie" crap; and besides, it was worth it for the scowl that passed across Lisa's face at having me take his attention away from her. Not that he'd been paying her much attention anyway. She really was wasting her time. For the life of me I couldn't see why she was persisting with this "we're meant to be together" business.

"You know that thing I gave you to read the other night?" she asked me, still bristling slightly at the interruption. "Have you finished with it yet?"

"Oh, no, I haven't. Sorry," I said. I did lay on the regret a bit, I have to confess. "I just haven't had the time. I really will get round to it soon, though, I promise."

Next to me, Gabriel played a showy arpeggio on the piano. "Ready, Mattie? And three four, one, two. . ."

Molly and I had a check-up at the dentist's the next morning. Mum dropped us off at school afterwards as the bell was going for break, and then decided she simply had to write us a note to hand in, excusing our absence. So then, of course, she had to get a pen and piece of paper from her bag, which she couldn't find. It must be wonderful to be so well organized. I sometimes think she's not safe to be let out by herself.

Moll got fed up of waiting for the note, and pushed off. "It's cool," she said, brushing off Mum's protestations. "We don't both need one. Mattie can hand it in at Reception."

I wasn't quite sure why I had to be the one to stand around like a lemon while Mum emptied the entire contents of her bag all over the back seat (having finally located it in the boot under a whole pile of Sainsbury's carrier bags full of the shopping she'd done while we were in the dentist's). Something to do with the privileges of being the eldest, I dare say.

"Honestly, Mum," I was saying, practically hopping from foot to foot with frustration. "I don't need a note now, I can bring it in tomorrow."

"Hiya, Mat," a voice said in my ear. "Been skiving off?"

I turned round. It was Jaz.

"Nah – been to the dentist. Mum's just writing me a note." I rolled my eyes to indicate the length of time this procedure was taking, and she grinned.

Mum straightened up, narrowly avoiding banging her head on the door frame, and smiled warmly at her. "Hello, Jasmilla! I haven't seen you for such a long time. How are you?"

"I'm fine thanks, Mrs Fry," Jaz replied politely. "How are you?"

"Oh, you know. Bearing up." Mum patted her tummy in a significant manner. "Everything seems to be going according to plan anyway, which is the main thing, isn't it? Mattie, darling, I really do think you're going to have to fetch that note in tomorrow. I can't seem to find a pen. It's a mystery – I'm sure I had one here somewhere. . ."

Jaz and I walked together across the damp tarmac of the playground.

"So how come you're only just coming in to school?" I asked her.

"Free periods. I don't have lessons till after break on Thursdays."

I hadn't even known. Time was when Jaz's school timetable was as familiar to me as my own. It just went to show how far apart we'd drifted without me even realizing the extent of it.

"The way Mum was faffing around out there, I didn't think I was going to get in till after break tomorrow," I said. I pushed open the door of the sixth-form block, and we went in and up the stairs. "Honest to God, she's seriously losing her marbles. Must be the hormones. . . What?"

Jaz had stopped dead, and was looking at me with a puzzled expression. "What's going on with your Mum?"

It hit me with a horrible thud. Like walking out in the road into the path of a bus. *Oh my God. I never got round to telling her.*

"Ummm . . . she's pregnant," I said. I felt terrible. "Look Jaz, I know I should have told you, I'm really sorry, I did mean to tell you, loads of times, but I just. . ." I didn't know what to say. She was still looking at me. The puzzlement had gone, and in its place was something different. Something hurt, unfathomable.

"Don't be daft," she said. "Why should you have told

me? It's not really any of my business, is it?" It wasn't just her expression. There was something strange about her voice, too.

"Well, no, maybe not, but . . . you're my mate. I tell you things. You tell me things. We tell each other things." I was beginning to sound like Lisa's wretched story.

"Course we do. Don't worry about it." She went down the stairs to the kitchen, with me following. I wanted to say, *but I am worrying about it*. I wanted to say, *talk to me*. But I didn't. "Fancy a coffee?" she asked me. "I could do with a caffeine hit, don't know about you."

"Erm . . . yeah, OK. Go on then." There was a pause while she filled the kettle and plugged it in, found two clean cups in the cupboard, then took out the jar of coffee with JAZ in big fluorescent pink letters scrawled across the address label stuck round its middle. "Jaz. . ."

"Mmm?" She turned round with the jar in her hand. "It'll have to be black. I thought there was some CoffeeMate in here, but someone must have nicked it."

Desperately, I caught hold of her sleeve. "I didn't deliberately not tell you, you know. About Mum. I tried to – that night I phoned you just as you were going into the cinema with Bex? When you were seeing that French film?"

She bit her lip. "That was ages ago. I'm sorry if I didn't listen then, but there've been loads of other opportunities. Why didn't you try again?" She said it really softly, almost sadly.

"I don't know. It was just. . ." I remembered something else I hadn't got round to telling her. "We're probably going to be moving, as well."

"Moving? What – away?" She looked shocked.

"I don't think so. Not *away*, away. Just to a bigger house. Because of – you know. The baby. Frankly, it sucks. All of it."

She put the jar down on the counter with a sudden thump. "See, this is what I don't get. There's all this major stuff been going on in your life, and I don't know anything about it."

"I know. It's like we were saying the other day, you've been hanging round with Bex so much, and—"

"Did we say that?" Her voice was suddenly sharp. "I don't remember us saying that. As I recall, what we said was that *you've* been hanging round with *Lisa* so much."

"Well, yeah, I know, that too, but. . ." She was right. I knew she was right. "But there's been a reason for that."

"Yeah – *Gabriel*." She said his name with scorn. "Have you any idea how much it pisses Bex off to hear you two giggling about him in corners the whole time, like a couple of twelve year olds?"

I was stung. "Well, yeah, I do actually. She told me. And I don't actually feel like that about him any more. And when I said there was a reason for me hanging out with Lisa, I didn't mean that."

"So what did you mean, then?"

I opened my mouth to answer her, then closed it again. What had I meant, exactly? After all, Jaz was right. Again. The original reason I'd got so chummy with Lisa so quickly was indeed Gabriel. And the reason I was still hanging out with her was because I was scared to death of the state she'd got herself into over him, and what she might do as a result. I just couldn't tell Jaz that, though. Don't ask me why. I just couldn't.

"I s'pose it was because of him at first," I admitted. "But c'mon, Jaz – it's not just been me not telling you things. I don't know much about what's been going on in *your* life lately, either."

"Well, my mum's not pregnant, and we're not about to move house," she said, slightly huffily. "And if she was and we were, you'd have been the first person I told. Especially if the whole thing was pissing me off as much as it seems to be pissing *you* off."

"Well, OK. Fair enough. But how about. . ." I cast around wildly for something ongoing that she hadn't updated me about for a while. "How about Patrice? How's things going with him?"

She sniffed. "Toast."

"What — you mean it's over?"

"Over, finished. History. He stopped answering my texts, and then emailed me to say he's already got a girlfriend."

"Bastard!" I tucked my arm through hers. "Well, there you go, then. You never told me about that, did you?"

"I guess not." Grudgingly.

"So we've both been as bad as each other, really, haven't we? Only I've been worse than you," I put in hastily. "But, look. This whole Gabriel thing with Lisa has got way out of hand. I don't like being around her any more — she's become like, I dunno. Weird. Avid."

"Avid?"

"Yeah. Avid. You know — greedy, like your dog when you put his dinner down for him?"

"Hmm. So what you're saying is. . ." She stroked her chin, musing. "Let me get this right. Lisa's become like Fang eating his dinner. Whoa. Scary."

Fang is a miniature Yorkshire terrier. I don't think I've ever come across a less scary dog in my life. I punched her on the arm, lightly. "Behave! Stop taking the piss! It's not funny, you know!"

She sniggered. "Yes, it is. Fang eating his dinner!" She repeated it, as if it was the funniest thing she'd ever heard, and I couldn't help joining in. You know how infectious it is when somebody else is laughing over something. It doesn't matter if it's stupid, it's still funny. And more to the point, it broke the tension between us. Things were back to normal again.

I suddenly remembered something. I bent down to my bag, and pulled out the blue plastic folder. "If you want any evidence of how Fang-like she's got, you want to take a look at this."

"What is it?" She put out her hand for it, and I hesitated. I'm not sure why. Some belated sense of loyalty to Lisa, perhaps.

"I'm not sure I should let you actually read it. But it's Lisa's – it's some kind of story thing. She wanted me to read it and tell her what I thought."

"Don't tell me, let me guess. *Gabriel!*" She made a kind of idiot-face, screwing up her nose and lifting her upper lip so her voice came out like a moron's.

"Exactly." I sniggered again. "Honestly, Jaz, it is such a pile of poo! It's like a comedy version of soft porn, all about his throbbing manhood, and satisfying his male lust in her soft feminine . . . what?" I became aware that Jaz had unscrewed her face and had opened her eyes wide at me in an expression of semi-alarm, whilst shaking her head almost imperceptibly from side to side. I turned round.

It had to be, didn't it? Lisa was standing behind me, her face expressionless. I had no idea how long she'd been standing there, but she'd clearly heard enough. Without saying a word, she turned on her heel and went up the stairs and out of the door.

I turned back to Jaz. In a simultaneous gesture of caught-out horror, our hands flew up to our mouths.

"Omigod," I said. "That's torn it."

The school bus home that afternoon was delayed because Moll was missing. I made the driver wait for her; he didn't want to, he was moaning about schedules and overtime and stuff, but I told him she was my little sister and I was responsible for her, and I'd report him to the authorities if he went without her and made her walk the nine kilometres home. It was just threatening to turn nasty when a dishevelled figure flung herself up the steps and on to the bus.

"The little sister, I presume," the driver sneered. "Thank bleedin' Christ for that. Do I have your permission to go now, missy? We do all have homes to go to, you know."

He pulled away with a hiss of air brakes, and I followed Moll as she stomped, muttering, down the aisle to the back.

"What kept you? I was getting desperate, I thought he was going to throw me off and make us both walk home!" She didn't answer. "Moll?"

She turned round. Her face was red, blotchy and stained with tears.

I was shocked. "Molly! What's the matter?"

She shook her head, and mumbled something I couldn't hear. All around us the usual home-going racket got under way as the bus swung along the lanes.

"Tell me! What's happened?"

I held her upper arm, but she shook me off and sat down, turning her face away from me.

"Nothing. Leave me alone, Mat. Just – butt out, OK?"

I couldn't sit next to her, or even near her; there was no room. I went back down the aisle and found a seat near the front, and when we got off the bus at the top of the hill down to Brandy Bay I tried again, but with no more luck than before. She just clamped her mouth tightly shut, and wouldn't even look at me.

By the time we'd got home, I'd had enough of the silent treatment.

"You've got to tell me what the problem is," I told her, as she took her front door key out of her purse and slotted it in the lock. "Things that make you this upset don't just go away by themselves, you know. And it's not the first time it's happened, is it?"

We stepped inside. She stood in the entrance, clasping her school bag to her chest like a shield, and eyed me warily. "I don't know what you mean."

"Yes, you do. You were spotted crying at school, remember? I've seen you looking upset, myself. I've heard you crying at night, with my own ears. What's going on?" She just carried on looking at me. I grasped her by the elbows and looked directly into her face. "What's going *on*?"

"Nothing." She gave a little sob, tried to shake me off. "*Nothing!* Mind your own business – piss *off*!"

With another wriggle she was free of me, but she dropped her school bag in the process. It fell to the slate flags of the hall floor, spilling its contents. She stood looking at it for a second, then with another sob she stepped across everything and dashed noisily up the stairs.

Not knowing the best thing to do, upset by her upsetness, I bent to retrieve her things. School books, homework, pencil case, empty plastic lunchbox, assorted paper hankies, funny little pink-haired troll thing Chloë had given her – I picked them all up and shoved them back in her bag, higgledy-piggledy.

I didn't see the note at first. It had fallen out of one the textbooks, a roughly-folded sheet of lined paper with ragged holes at the top, torn from a ring-bound notepad. Her name, misspelt, was scribbled in heavy blue biro on the outside. *MOLY FRY*. I opened it, guiltily. Afterwards, I was glad I did. Glad but horrified.

Your a manky ginger fartface, it said. Ginger. Ginger

stinkbom. You should have bin killd at birth. Ginger kids stink like pigsh—

Well, never mind. You get the gist. I'd discovered the reason for Molly's lateness to the bus, and dishevelment, and tears. It was all, apparently, because of the colour of her hair.

Chapter Sixteen

"You should have told me." I was sitting on her bed, holding her hand. "I knew something was up ages ago. You should have said you were being bullied."

She shrugged, wordlessly.

"Anyway, you're not even ginger," I went on. "I could understand it if you were. I mean, being ginger – whoa! Hanging offence. But you're not. You're – you're strawberry blonde."

A strand of her hair, bright and shiny as a new penny, had escaped her scrunchie and hung limply around her face. I touched it, gently, and she gave a weak little smile. "I know. I'm pathetic."

"*You're* pathetic? How does that work? You don't think the goon who wrote this note is the pathetic one?"

"I'm pathetic for letting it get to me."

"Moll." I took her other hand, held both of hers in mine. "It would have got to anybody. Just out of interest, how long's it been going on?"

She wrinkled her nose, considering. "Dunno exactly. A few months, I guess."

"A few *months*? Why didn't you tell me? When did it start?" I felt furiously protective, mad at the moron who'd done this to her. And like I'd somehow let her down, that I should have been there for her.

"At the end of last term. Before the holidays. I thought they'd forget all about it over the summer, but as soon as school started again, so did they."

"*They?* You mean, there's more than one?" I was surprised at the strength of my feeling, the rage I felt at these unknown people who'd been making my little sister's life a misery without me even knowing about it.

"Lauren Postle, in my year. She's the main one. She's always picking on somebody for something. Before me it was Jason Brown, for being dyslexic. The rest are just her hangers-on."

"Well, she won't be doing it any more. Trust me," I said grimly. I didn't have a clue who this Lauren person was, but it hardly mattered. "I'll have a little word in her ear. And if that doesn't work, I might just get Andy to have a little word in her ear, too. Having beefy mates in the Upper Sixth comes in handy at times."

A look of apprehension flitted across her face. "I don't want any fuss. . ."

"There won't be any fuss, don't worry. It will all be

totally fuss-free." I looked into her face. "I still can't understand why you didn't tell me about it."

Another shrug. "Didn't think there was any point."

"Of course there was a point! You were being bullied!"

"But would you have listened? Would you have heard? You've been so wrapped up in your stuff lately. I didn't think you had time for anybody else."

I stared at her. "What do you mean, wrapped up in my stuff?"

"Oh, come on, Mat. You know what I mean. Lisa – your new best friend. And *Gabriel*." Why was it everybody recently seemed to say his name with such contempt?

"Lisa's not my new best friend. She's. . . Well, never mind. But I hardly have anything to do with her these days. And I'm over Gabriel. I have been for ages. It was just a silly crush."

"So what about that pile of crap you wrote about him, then?"

"What pile of crap?" Had she found my diary, been reading the stuff I'd written way back at the beginning? *Reasons for Adoring Gabriel*. . . Jeez. How embarrassing, if so.

"That story thing. Or whatever it was."

I nearly laughed out loud with relief. "You mean, that thing in the blue plastic folder? That wasn't mine,

246

it was Lisa's! She wanted me to read it, and tell her what I thought."

"Bloody hell." Molly grinned suddenly. "Thank goodness for that. I thought you'd flipped. So what did you tell her?"

"I didn't. I haven't got round to giving it back to her yet, it's still in my school bag."

The grin faded as quickly as it had arrived. Moll looked down and began to trace the abstract pattern of the duvet cover with a finger. "Even so. I still didn't think you'd have been bothered about my stupid problems. You've been really weird lately."

"Have I? What about?"

"About all kinds of things. Mum, and the baby. I know it was a shock, but – well, it's happened, hasn't it? There's nothing we can do about. We should have been talking about it, you and me, but you made it plain you didn't want to. You just seemed to want to block it out. And there was that thing on Geoffrey's birthday, when you went properly ballistic over those house details. I mean, we were only looking at them, for heaven's sake. And it's not like Mum and Geoffrey haven't been talking for ages about the house being too small once the baby's here. . ." She stopped for a moment, looked up at me. "It's like, you're just not aware of what's going on with the rest of us any more. Like you've stopped being a proper part of the family."

That really hurt. "Not part of the family? How can you say that?"

"Well, OK, maybe that's a bit harsh, but it's how it's felt. You just don't seem interested in what's going on round here. Bloody hell, Mat – I even talked to *Rupert* about the bullying thing, rather than you!"

"Did you?" Every word she uttered made me feel even worse. "And did he help?"

"He did, actually. Course, he was bullied himself, so he understood how it felt."

"We never bullied him! Not really. Not like *proper* bullying. It was only a bit of name-calling, at worst."

"I didn't mean us. I was talking about when he was bullied at school, before Mum and Geoffrey got married."

There was a small silence.

"I'd forgotten about that," I confessed.

"Do you still hate him?" she asked me suddenly.

I was taken aback. "*Hate* him? No, I don't hate him. I'm not sure I ever hated him, exactly. Let's face it, though, he's pretty hard to actually like."

"No, he's not. Not if you make an effort. He's just a person, like anybody else. He's had to cope with just as much shit in his life as we have. More, probably, if you consider his mum having been so ill and dying, and all that," she mused. "Maybe that's why he was so upset about Colin. Perhaps he was his last link to his mum."

I didn't know what she meant. "Why was he upset about Colin?"

"Because he died, didn't he? A month or so ago?" She looked up at me then, really looked at me. "Oh my God. You mean you didn't know?"

"No, I didn't!" I felt ridiculously upset. Not because of Rupert's rat having died – that would have been daft. I don't even like rats. But because Rupert had loved him and would have been upset, really upset, and I hadn't even been aware of this little drama going on under the same roof as me; and the fact I hadn't been aware just seemed to prove Molly's point, that somehow, somewhere along the line, I seemed to have stopped being a proper part of the family. That was the really upsetting thing.

On the bus to school the next day, I thought about what Molly had said. If I needed any more evidence that my friendship with Lisa was doomed, this was it. My family had always been so important; it's what got me through those dark days after leaving Dad and Manchester, the sense of our little family unit pulling together. True, it had majorly wobbled when Geoffrey and Rupert had come on the scene, but even then I'd had a perception of what I know now for sure: that their arrival didn't threaten to pull the family asunder, it simply heralded a redistribution of the balance. In fact, if anyone had endangered the whole thing it had been me, with my dogged refusal to accept . . . well, whatever it was. Change, I guess. And now here I was, on the verge of doing the same thing, with my refusal to face up to things and my lack of involvement in what was going on under my nose. And to make matters worse, I'd been doing all that in favour of the unbalanced, unhealthy thing that my friendship with Lisa had become.

What I couldn't understand was why I was finding it so hard to drop her. It wasn't like she'd been part of my life for very long, why couldn't I just ease her out of it? The answer, I guess, is that things were more complicated than that. I necessarily saw a lot of her around school, mainly because we were in several lessons together, lessons without Jaz, and Lisa seemed to have developed this knack of sitting next to me regardless of whether I turned up first or she did, or whether I was talking to anybody; she'd just kind of slide into the seat next to me as if it was her natural place. People had started talking of Lisa and me in the same breath, I'd noticed, bracketing our names together the way they do with best mates. Mattie and Lisa. You 'n' Lisa. Are you 'n' Lisa going to Seb's party next week? Have you 'n' Lisa done that essay yet? It used to be Mattie 'n' Jaz. I missed those days. How ironic that Jaz had warned me about Lisa from the start, about how she'd done something similar with her: got too intense, tried to take her over.

The main problem was that, quite apart from being worried about Lisa and her weird behaviour, I felt sorry for her. She didn't seem to have many other friends. None, in fact, or certainly none whose company she sought out anywhere near as frequently as mine. No matter that her feelings for Gabriel had reached bizarrely epic proportions long ago; she was obviously suffering over it, and anyway who was I to judge? She hadn't forced me to join in. At the end of the day she was just a lonely girl with a crush who'd wanted to be my friend. I couldn't just flatly cut her out of my life, it would have been unkind and unnecessary; and anyway, there was the matter of *Grease*. I was really enjoying it now Andy had turned up and was Teen Angel to my Frenchy. I was hanging out with him rather than Lisa at rehearsals, I was finally getting to grips with the singing thanks to Gabriel's endless patience, and all the acting stuff was a real blast. I didn't want to have to give it all up in order to remove Lisa from my life. Besides, I didn't see why I should have to. I would just have to think of ways I could avoid even more contact with her without being hurtful, and in time she'd doubtless get the message and move on, just as she had with Jaz last year. (OK, so that time she'd moved on to me, but hey. . .)

To begin with, though, I thought it might be a good idea to try and make amends over her story. Although in some ways not talking to her any more was what I wanted to happen, it wasn't exactly *how* I wanted it to happen. Leaving things like this cast me firmly in the role of the villain: the nasty one, the slagger-offer. The bitch. Which, let's face it, she'd have been entitled to think, under the circumstances. Fair dos – I felt guilty about it. And quite apart from anything else, I still had the wretched story sitting in my school bag, squatting there like some evil ugly toad in a children's fairy story, casting a spell, a hundred-year curse or something. All in all, I needed to make my peace with Lisa and get shot of it.

Ironically, it took me ages to catch her by herself. Typical, isn't it; on any other day she'd have been following me around like Mary's little lamb, yet the day I *wanted* to speak to her, she seemed to be trying to evade me. Finally, I caught up with her in the sixth-form block at lunch time. I was a bit late going in for lunch, and she was standing in the dining area with a tray, scanning the room to work out where she was going to sit.

I put a hand on her arm. "Lisa. . ."

She jumped, and looked at me as if she thought I was going to bite her. "What do you want?"

I laughed a carefree, merry laugh that didn't at all

reflect how I was feeling. "Don't be like that! I just wanted a chat, that's all."

"Yeah, well . . . I'm just about to have lunch."

I glanced at her tray. It held a pixie-sized glass bowl of salad, an orange, and a glass of water. "Is that your lunch? Jeez – I hope you're going to have a big tea."

It was meant as a joke, but she pulled a face and swung away from me, muttering something I couldn't catch.

"Lisa . . . please! I wanted to say sorry."

"Sorry for what?"

"For being horrible about your story. I know you overheard what I said to Jaz the other day. It was mean of me, and I'm really sorry."

"Mmmph."

That's what she said. A noise, not a word. I pressed on, aware that people at the neighbouring tables had stopped their own conversations and were listening to ours. I tried to keep my voice down.

"I really am sorry. Honestly. I know it means a lot to you, what with your feelings about Gabriel and all. I shouldn't have said what I did, and I apologize. Whole-heartedly."

I paused, waited for her to say that's OK, it doesn't matter, I forgive you. That's what people are supposed to say after an apology, isn't it? That's what always happens in books, and films. Only Lisa obviously hadn't read the books, or seen the films, because what she did was put her tray down on a nearby table, carefully, as if scared she might drop it, and then turn back to me and slap me, surprisingly hard – so hard I reeled from the blow – across the face. After which she crumpled to the ground in a dead faint. I say to the ground, but actually Andy, who had been seated at one of the aforementioned neighbouring tables, jumped to his feet and caught her deftly, like a wicketkeeper fielding a tricky delivery, just at the moment she slid to the floor.

It turned out she hadn't eaten any breakfast, or supper, or lunch the day before. Or pretty much anything of any significant calorific value for the past few weeks. I sat with her in the medical room, guiltily holding her hand while she recounted all of this to the school nurse, obediently answering her questions with bowed head and submissive voice.

"I was too fat," Lisa was saying, over and over.

"Lovey, you can't just stop eating. The body has a way of saying enough's enough, and that's what yours has just done."

"I thought he'd love me if I was thin."

The nurse looked at me, raising her eyebrows quizzically. "Boy trouble?" I nodded. "If he doesn't love you the way you are, he's not worth it. No boy is worth making yourself ill over. And besides, what boy is going to want to go out with somebody who's obsessive about their eating?"

And not just their eating, I thought to myself. *If only she knew. . .*

After she'd gone, leaving us to it while she "made some phone calls" (to Lisa's mum, presumably), we talked. Or rather, I talked, and Lisa wept. After a bit I gave up talking, and let her cry.

"I've been so stupid," she sobbed. "Starving myself to try and make Gabriel look at me."

"But you haven't been throwing up as well, have you? Promise me you haven't."

"No, no. I told you before. I'm so useless I couldn't even have a proper eating disorder."

I started to reply before I realized it was her attempt at a joke. A pretty tasteless one, but a joke nonetheless.

"You're not useless. Come here." I enfolded her in a hug. It was one of relief, that finally she'd been forced to face up to the eating thing, that somebody else knew about it. She returned my hug, warmly.

"You're such a good friend, Mattie. I'm sorry I hit you. I don't mind about the story, honestly. You were right, it was a pile of poo – even I knew that. I guess I just wanted you to tell me it was good, even though I knew it wasn't. I just so want some romance in my life."

I cast around for something to say to her that would

cheer her up. "You know what? You should have seen Andy, catching you when you fainted. I don't think I've ever seen anything so romantic!"

But she just shook her head sadly. "I meant romance with Gabriel. Anyway, it's no good with Andy. It's you he fancies. Everybody knows that."

He was waiting for me outside the medical room when I left Lisa.

"She OK now?" he asked me, indicating the door with his head.

"Seems to be. She's just waiting for her mum to come and fetch her home." I fiddled with the buckle on my bag. "It's partly my fault. I knew she hadn't been eating properly. I've known for ages."

"How can it be your fault?"

"I should have stopped her. I should have said something to her about it."

"Oh, right. You reckon she'd have listened to you, then?"

"I don't know. Maybe not." I looked up at him, silently. There weren't words to express how bad I felt about the whole thing. Lisa's words rang in my ears – *you're such a good friend, Mattie. . .* I knew damn well I was anything but.

"You daft thing. Why do you think you're responsible for everybody else's problems?"

He put his arms round me and gave me a hug, a proper friend's hug, and as I subsided against him I thought how much I wanted to stay like that for ever, enfolded in Andy's arms, letting him make me feel better about things. Even though I had no right to feel better, about anything.

I didn't stay feeling better for long. In that way life has of kicking you in the teeth several times over, Molly and I got home from school that afternoon to find a note from Geoffrey on the kitchen table, telling us that Mum was in hospital having a suspected miscarriage.

Chapter Seventeen

We rang for a cab to take us to the hospital, and all the way there Molly held my hand tightly, as if it was the only thing keeping her tethered to this planet and she might be whisked away into outer space if she let go.

"She is going to be all right, isn't she?" she kept saying to me. Kept whispering. Her face was ashen, her eyes huge and dark with anxiety, her bottom lip trembling.

"Of course she is. She's going to be fine." I heard myself say the words over and over. I didn't really believe them, was trying to reassure myself as much as Moll. How could I know whether she was going to be fine? I know nothing about pregnancy; *any* pregnancy, far less this one. After Mum had told us about it, I'd been so wrapped up in my own feelings about everything I hadn't even bothered enquiring any further. I wasn't even certain how far on Mum was – five months, six? I didn't have the faintest clue how her pregnancy had been progressing, or even whether a miscarriage at this stage could be fatal for the mother as well as the baby. All I could do was cling on to Molly's hand and murmur my soothing meaningless words, and hope.

We arrived at the hospital in a daze, spoke to somebody at reception who directed us with detached efficiency, went up several floors in a lift – which stopped all the while with an increasingly irritating ping to let people on and off amidst polite shuffling and careful avoidance of eye contact – and finally hurried along miles of endless identical corridor. At last we turned a corner, and through double doors into a ward. It was large and brightly lit. Curtains in pretty pastel shades were drawn back around white-blanketed beds, each containing a woman either holding a baby, surrounded by beaming visitors holding a baby, or asleep with a nearby aquarium-like crib holding a baby. Everywhere I looked there were flowers: vases of flowers, baskets of flowers, flowers contained within little china bootees or teddies in pink and blue, or amidst bobbing, helium-filled metallic balloons with *It's a boy!* and *She's here!* printed triumphantly on their fat shiny surfaces. The whole atmosphere was one of joy and celebration and calm milky serenity, utterly at odds with the reason Molly and I were here. A shaft of something sharp and painful sliced through me, that here were all these mothers with their new babies, and our own mother wasn't going to have. . .

"Yes, girls? Can I help?"

I turned. A large black nurse in a blue uniform was smiling at us. "Oh . . . no . . . I think we've come to the wrong ward."

"This is post-natal. Who've you come to see?"

"My mum. Alice Fry. Horton, I mean – Alice Horton."

"Ah, yes. Alice. She's down at the end. Don't worry, honey." She smiled again. "She's doing just fine."

Amazingly, astonishingly, she was. Just fine. She was sitting up in bed, with Geoffrey sitting on one side and Rupert on the other, and dressed in one of those disgusting hospital gowns that do up at the back and show your bum when you walk. She was wan and tired-looking, but she was – well, fine. I wondered, briefly, why Rupert was here, until I remembered. It was Friday: he was home for the weekend. Time was I'd have resented his presence – his, and his father's. Now, I was just glad Mum had had some support, hadn't had to suffer whatever it was she'd gone through alone.

She looked up as Molly and I approached, and smiled.

"Hello, darlings. Have you come all this way by yourselves?"

"We got a taxi," Molly told her. "We had to take some money from the telephone box. I hope you don't mind."

"Of course I don't mind! It's lovely to see you both."

"So – what happened?" Molly looked from Mum to Geoffrey.

"I had a bit of a scare," Mum started. Geoffrey took her hand, and patted it in a there-there manner.

"I came back from fetching Rupert from the station to find Alice in the bathroom," he carried on. "She'd been bleeding, and I'm afraid I panicked and whisked her off here."

"You did the right thing, darling. You heard what the doctor said – better safe than sorry."

"So – does that mean everything's OK? What about the baby?" It was only when I asked the question that I realized I'd been holding my breath, not daring to put into words what I'd been fearing.

"Everything's completely OK, and the baby's absolutely tickety-boo," Geoffrey said. "No harm done at all."

He and Mum looked at each other with love, and I felt relief well up inside me. It came out as a kind of little gasping sob. I put my hand up to my mouth, to try and push it back in, and Rupert got up from the chair he'd been sitting on.

"Are you all wight? Here, sit down."

"Thanks." I sat down, heavily, and he thumped my shoulder in a clumsy gesture of consolation.

"Bit of a shock," he said.

Geoffrey nodded earnestly. "I'll say. For everybody. Girls, I'm so sorry I left that note. I realize perhaps I shouldn't have been so specific, it must have been very frightening for you, but it was the only. . ."

"It's OK," I assured him. Typical Geoffrey, making a speech at a time like this. Bless him. "We understand, don't we, Moll?"

"You did what you thought was best at the time," Molly said. "And you had to let us know what was going on."

"And the main thing," Rupert chipped in, "is that your mum's all wight. Isn't it?"

I took her free hand in mine. "Of course it is. And the baby. Don't forget the baby."

She squeezed my hand, and our eyes met. "Thank you, Mattie," she whispered.

"She was on a post-natal ward?" Jaz said. "With all the new mums and their babies? Christ. That's a bit harsh, isn't it? What if it hadn't been a false alarm after all, and she'd actually lost the baby?"

"I don't know," I said. "Maybe she'd have been put on another ward then. But the point is, she didn't lose it. It's all fine."

"Is it?" She looked closely at me. "Is it really? Last time I heard, you weren't a happy bunny about it at all."

"Well, I am now," I declared. "Everything's cool."

"Everything?"

"Everything."

"The baby?"

"Yeah."

"Moving house?"

"Hmm . . . depends on the house. But yeah. I guess."

"You 'n' me?" She looked even closer, right into my face. "Lisa?"

"Hell, yeah!" I grinned. "Lisa's fine too. Isn't it odd how just about everything in your life can be giving you grief one day, and the next it all seems to be sorted?"

Even Molly's life appeared to be back on an even keel. I didn't even need to have the promised word in the ear of the poisonous Laura, or Lauren, or whatever her name was. Molly just seemed much brighter, lighter in spirits, and when I asked her how things were with You-Know-What – cocking a meaningful eyebrow – she smiled and said, oh that, no worries, it's all over. I didn't know what had happened since she'd come clean to me about everything, but it seemed to have done the trick. Perhaps nothing had happened at all;

maybe just telling me about it had been enough for her to feel able to cope with it. I don't know.

But one thing I did know was that she wasn't about to keep stuff like that to herself in the future. Something strange seemed to have happened since Mum's scare with the baby, and it had happened to all of us, not just Moll. All of us at home, I mean. The Fry-Hortons. We seemed to have reached a new kind of understanding with each other. I don't mean that in a cheesy, icky, falling-on-each-other's-necks kind of way, but just that we . . . I don't know. I can't explain. I guess it felt like we were all pulling together more on things, rather than pulling against each other. Though I have a sneaking suspicion the others might have been doing that anyway, and it was just me who had been the fly in the ointment.

All in all, everything seemed to have shifted down to a more comfortable level. Until the last *Grease* rehearsal before Christmas.

The rehearsals finished at the beginning of December. It seemed rather early, but Lynda Pym was going off to Canada for a month to spend Christmas and the New Year with family out there. Mavis and Percy had suggested having a little party at the final rehearsal – "a bit of a do" – so we could all wish each other merry Crimbo, say bon voyage to Lynda, that kind of thing.

Oh yeah, and to bid Gabriel farewell. He was off to do his ski instructor thing in the New Year, and would be jacking in the accompanying. Funny thing was, I'd totally forgotten about it.

Lisa hadn't, though. I saw her face when Mavis mentioned it.

"Of course, we'll have to give dear Gabriel a good send-off," Mavis had said to us all, beaming. "He's been a godsend. I'll make some of my special sausage rolls. What kind of food are you likely to be having in France, dear?"

Lisa flinched as if somebody had stuck a knife in her back, and her face twisted. *Oh God*, I thought, with a sinking heart. *Please don't let her start all that eating stuff again.* Although, in truth, I didn't really know whether she'd actually stopped it, as I'd managed to avoid spending any time alone with her since her fainting episode at school. I'm not saying I'd been ignoring her – I wouldn't have been that horrible. I'd just made sure there were other people around when we'd spoken to each other. It seemed safest all round.

So the final rehearsal came at last, and people arrived at the hall with bottles of wine and plates of goodies covered with tinfoil and clingfilm. Coincidentally, Andy and I got there at exactly the same moment. It was dark outside the hall, and as I approached the entrance another figure detached itself from the shadows, making me jump.

"Evening."

"Oh, hi Andy! God, I didn't see you there!"

He waved a bottle of red in my direction. "This is a good idea, isn't it? Don't know about you, but I'm going to miss these sessions."

"What, drinking? I'm sure you'll find plenty of that going on over Christmas, if you look hard enough."

"No, I meant . . . oh, I see. Joke." He seemed oddly grave.

"What's up?"

"Me? No, nothing. Hello, Lisa."

She was tottering up the path in some kind of spike-heeled footwear. It was too dark to see what, exactly.

"Mattie." She clutched at my arm, urgently. "I've got to talk to you."

"Umm . . . OK." She bent to fiddle with her heel, and I pulled a Help Me face to Andy across her back. Unfortunately, he didn't seem to see it in the darkness and went on inside.

Lisa straightened up. "I've got to do something about Gabriel tonight. It's my last chance before he goes away."

I groped for something to say, something neutral, soothing. "You could always ask him for his email address. Say you'd like to keep in touch – pen pals, kind of thing."

"I don't want to be his *pen pal*!" she wailed. "I want *him*! I'm *desperate*!"

At the bottom of the path, I could make out the majestic figure of Lynda Pym coming towards us, laden with baskets and bags that clinked gently as she walked.

"Ssh!" I hissed to Lisa, flapping my hands. "Keep it down!"

"Good evening, ladies," Lynda greeted us. The moment she entered the building Lisa was off again.

"I've been in agony! I can't bear the thought of never seeing him again! I just can't *bear* it!"

I felt the familiar prickle of irritation. "Well, sorry to pee on your chips, but I somehow don't think you're going to cop off with him tonight. Not here, in front of everybody – I don't think it's going to be that kind of party."

"I'm not intending to cop off with him," she replied, wounded. "I'm not that crass. I've decided I'm going to stop him going away."

Oh, right. Course you are. He's going to take one look at you over one of Mavis's sausage rolls and a glass of warm white wine, and realize what he's been missing all these months.

You know what? It was on the tip of my tongue to

say it, the words were actually forming in my mouth. The only thing that stopped me was the man himself. Gabriel, coming up the path. He gave us both a warm smile, and my stomach gave a little flip. I still fancied him, despite what I'd said. Of course I did. He was probably the most beautiful bloke I'd ever seen in my life – how could I not fancy him? But mine was a normal, female-responding-to-male kind of fancying, not this hot, obsessive, stalkerish infatuation of Lisa's.

"Gabriel," I said, following him in. "I've been meaning to ask you. . ."

I wittered on about something or another, it didn't matter what, anything to get away from Lisa. I was aware of her still standing outside, giving me evils behind my back in all likelihood, but I didn't care. I'd had just about all I could take of her neediness.

After the rehearsal, we all gathered around the trestle tables that had been set up at one end of the room. They were laden with sandwiches, bowls of crisps, plates of mince pies, and yes, Mavis's famous sausage rolls. There were bottles of wine and cans of beer, and neat rows of up-ended glasses, waiting to be filled. The hall had been festooned with paper chains and strings of tinsel, and somebody had brought along a CD player and put on a recording of Christmas carols. It all seemed a bit early for all that kind of thing, to be honest, but it was nonetheless very jolly.

As the level of conversation rose, I snuck a look over at Lisa. She'd come to the rehearsal dressed in a tight black slit skirt, fishnet tights and the spike-heeled shoes. This ensemble was topped with the low-cut red and black corset top she'd bought when we'd gone shopping together. Her outfit had caused some stir amongst the Year Nines, who'd nudged each other and tittered pointedly when she'd removed her coat, but she'd just shrugged contemptuously.

"We *are* having a party afterwards," she'd said. "Speaking personally, I try to make an effort for parties."

She did look pretty hot, there was no doubt about it, but as I'd said, it simply wasn't that kind of party. Everybody else was dressed in casual clothes – jeans, tees, open-necked shirts. If I'd been dressed the way Lisa was I'd have felt embarrassed, overdressed, out of place.

"Do us a favour," I said to Andy, sotto voce. "Go and chat to Lisa."

He looked over at her. "Why?"

"I just. . ." I couldn't think of a valid reason, other than that I felt sorry for her. "Aww, go on." I leant against him slightly, nudging him with my shoulder. "Go and have a chat. I'll come over and join you in a mo'."

Obediently, he drifted over, and I took a handful of crisps and put them in my mouth. Gabriel was standing opposite me, watching us, clutching a bottle of lager. I smiled at him, and he smiled back.

"You've got a fan there," he told me.

"Who? Andy? Nah, we're just mates."

"If you say so." He grinned again. "He looks pretty smitten to me. Rumour has it he only started coming along here because of you."

I felt the flush rise up my face. "I don't understand why everyone's saying that. Why couldn't he just come along because he wanted to be in *Grease*? He's actually a really good singer."

"Yeah, he is. You're right. Sorry – no offence."

What was the matter with me? He was only making an observation, there'd been no malice in it. I sighed. "That's OK. None taken. Are you going already?" He'd put his drink down and was making as if leaving.

"No, I'm just going outside for a smoke."

"Can I come too? I could do with some fresh air."

"Sure."

As we left the hall together it struck me that only a few weeks ago I'd have killed for the opportunity to be alone with Gabriel. Well, maybe not killed exactly, but pretty damn close. Now, though, I was more realistic. I knew there was no chance he'd ever have feelings for me other than ordinary normal ones to do with being his sister's friend. At that moment I wished Lisa realized the same thing. How much easier life would be if she did. For her, I mean – not just for me.

"So, are you looking forward to going to France?" I asked him.

"You bet. It's going to be immense." I saw the tip of his cigarette glow red in the dark as he took a drag.

"How long are you planning to be out there, then?"

"As long as the snow lasts. Late April, early May? Then I'm going to stay with my grandmother for the summer. She's got a house in Provence, it's amazing."

"Is it a big house?"

"Not especially. Just a really pretty area. We used to go there every summer holidays when Bex and I were little. The smell at night is wonderful – wild herbs, lavender. It's the smell of my childhood." He took another drag. "You ought to get Bex to take you guys out there some time. You'd love it."

I took a deep breath. "Gabriel?"

"Mm-hm?"

"You do know about Lisa, don't you?"

"What about her?"

"Never mind." It was no good, I couldn't do it. It would have been a kind of betrayal, even though I wouldn't have intended it as such.

There was a pause.

"You mean, the thing she's got for me?" he said gently.

Damn. He'd known all along.

"Yeah," I muttered.

"Yes, I know about it." Another pause. "I'm really sorry, Mattie. I can't help who I like and don't like. Not that I don't like her," he added hastily. "Just. . ."

"Not in that way," I finished for him.

"I'm sorry," he said again. "I know she's a mate of yours and all."

"Oh, God, no, that's OK, I mean. . ." God! What was he thinking? That this was some kind of "my friend fancies you" set-up? "No, I was just wondering if you might. . ." Might what? Have a quiet word in her ear and tell her to back off? Tell her there's no way in a month of Sundays he'd ever fancy her, no matter how thin she made herself? Yeah, like *that* would help the situation. . . "Doesn't matter," I muttered, but I don't think he even noticed.

"Anyway, I'm not looking for any kind of relationship right now," he went on. "Not since Felicity. . . And after France I'm off to uni, so – you know."

"Yeah. I see." Another embarrassed pause. "Where is it you're going, again?" I realized that, after all this time, I didn't know. I bet Lisa did, though. She'd probably have been able to give me a rundown of his A level grades, too.

"To uni? Warwick." He took a last drag, threw his cigarette down and ground it out with his heel. "Shall

272

we go back in? I don't know about you, but I'm freezing my butt off out here."

"Sure."

As we went inside he put a hand on the small of my back and said in my ear, "Go on. He's waiting for you, look!"

Andy was still standing by the table with Lisa, nodding at what she was saying but clearly not listening, his eyes flicking round the room.

"Shut up!" I gave Gabriel a playful dig in the ribs with my elbow. "Fool!"

"You OK?" Andy asked, as I reached him. He picked up a bottle and proffered it in my direction. "Glass of white?"

"Mm, yes please."

"What was that all about?" Lisa asked me. She seemed odd, on edge. Her face was flushed, her voice shrill. "You and Gabriel, outside?"

"Nothing," I said. I took the glass from Andy. "It was nothing, honestly."

"What were you talking about?" she persisted. "What did he say to you?"

Just at that moment there was a sudden flash and some sparks, and one of the big lights went out, plunging the hall into semi-darkness. Everybody made that ooh-ing noise they always do on these sort of occasions.

"Oh no!" Lynda said, crestfallen. "Oh, what a shame! What a way to end proceedings – we can barely see each other!"

Somebody piped up there was a spare bulb in the kitchen, and somehow Gabriel got volunteered to change it.

"Shouldn't somebody turn all the lights off at the mains?" Andy observed. "Pretty dangerous, otherwise."

"It's all right," Percy told him. "The ones in here are on a separate fuse to the rest of the building. We can leave the light on in the kitchen for him to see by – plenty of light coming through the hatch, look."

"Do you mind, dear?" Lynda asked Gabriel anxiously.

"Course not. It can be my last deed for the St Mark's Players," he said.

Everybody laughed, and somebody went to fetch a stepladder from behind the stage.

Amongst the hubbub, Lisa grabbed my arm. "What were you talking to him about out there?" she said again. "Tell me!"

I tried to shake her off but she was hanging on like a limpet. "I told you. Nothing," I insisted. "Nothing interesting, anyway. Him going to France. His gran's house. Boring stuff. Small talk."

Under the defunct light, Gabriel was climbing up the ladder.

"I don't believe you," Lisa said. Her face was set, her voice held a note of hysteria. "I think you were trying to seduce him."

"*Seduce* him?" I laughed. I couldn't help it, the idea was just so ludicrous. So was the word. I didn't think anybody said seduce any more. "Don't be daft! Lisa, come on. Get a grip. You've got to stop this – it's not doing you any good!"

"I can't stop it!" she burst out loudly, all of a sudden. "I can't! I *can't*!" Beside herself, she put her hands to her face, then her head, pulling at her hair, her face contorted with the strength of whatever it was that was going on inside her brain.

People abruptly stopped talking, turned to look at her, staring, alarmed, wondering what the outburst was all about.

And so it was that the entire membership of the St Mark's Players – cast, backstage crew, producer, hangers-on, the lot – witnessed that nice girl Lisa, who never said boo to a goose, deliberately launch herself across the room and collide full tilt with the ladder that had Gabriel perched at the top, knocking it off balance with a scream of indescribable, unholy anguish.

I'll never forget the sound of that scream, not as long as I live. Never forget the sight of the ladder toppling, in dreadful slow motion, never forget Gabriel's expression of dismay, turning to horror as he felt himself falling, clutching vainly at a strand of tinsel as he went, nor the dreadful hollow thud as he hit the ground.

There was a moment's appalled, horrified silence as everybody else's eyes followed all this, disbelievingly watched the action unfold. Then Lisa flung herself to the floor with him, clutching at him, weeping uncontrollably.

"I said I'd stop you going," she was sobbing, over and over. "I said I'd stop you."

Chapter Eighteen

So in the end, she was right. She'd stopped him. He'd broken his leg when he fell from the ladder, so that was the end of him going away to be a ski instructor. General consensus was it was a miracle he hadn't broken his neck, or that could have been the end of him, period.

It was a bad break, in two separate places, involving surgery and metal plates and whatnot. I can still see him now, lying there on the floor in semi-darkness, with his leg buckled underneath him at a sickening angle and Lisa half draped across him, howling like a banshee. They looked for all the world like a tableau from some gruesome Gothic melodrama. In some ways it was probably her perfect moment, the one she'd dreamed of for so long: the two of them, together, held in the spotlight of everybody else's attention.

There was a moment of total, utter stillness. Then the hall was filled with urgent action, calls for an ambulance, gentle hands lifting Lisa up and sitting her down on a hastily fetched chair with a glass of water, others tending to Gabriel, talking to him, checking his vital signs (or whatever the phrase is), and covering him with a blanket before the paramedics arrived to take over and bear him away.

Lisa was only partially right, though. She'd stopped him being a ski instructor, sure enough, but she didn't stop him going away. He flew out to France early in the New Year, broken leg, crutches, metal plates and all, to stay with his grandmother in Provence. That was a few weeks ago now. The last Bex told us, the local doctors were pleased with the way his leg was healing, and he'd got a job teaching English in a local primary school. His grandmother was acting as his chauffeur as well as his housekeeper, driving him around and generally looking after him, and all in all he was having a brilliant time, despite the broken leg. Apparently he's enjoying it so much, Bex says he's not sure he's going to bother coming back to go to uni after all. It's not like he needs to, really; he's got a job, and already speaks fluent French, so what more could a degree add, when it comes down to it?

I suppose the church hall must have been cleared up at some point, the remnants of our party tidied away, the floor swept. The light bulb changed, even. For all I know, the debris might still be there now, weeks after it all happened. I wouldn't know, because I never went back to the hall, nor the *Grease* rehearsals. I felt really bad about leaving them in the lurch, but I just couldn't face returning after Christmas to the inevitable post-mortems and gossip, the what-was-going-ons and why-did-she-do-its; and the more time goes by, the harder it's going to be to go back. Andy keeps telling me I should. He says nobody even mentions what happened any more. He tells me Roxanne, aka Drooly from the Year Nines, is Lisa's replacement as the new Rizzo, and one of her mates (Giggly or Starey, I can't remember which) is standing in as Frenchy until, as he puts it, I see sense and haul my arse back there. I haven't got the heart to tell him the jury's still out on my arse's location, at least for the time being. Maybe in a month or two, when everything has blown over. Who knows.

See, I feel responsible. Oh, I know deep down that I couldn't have known what Lisa was about to do – it was plain even *she* didn't plan it, it was a spur-of-the-moment thing – and even if I had somehow known, how could I have prevented it? By hurling myself in her path, between her and Gabriel, perched up on the ladder? I don't think so. But knowing that doesn't stop this sense of guilt. Perhaps I could have helped to prevent it; maybe I should have taken Lisa's growing obsession more seriously, tried to do something about it, rather than being repelled by it and distancing myself from her.

And one thing I know for sure. I certainly shouldn't have gone with Gabriel when he went outside for that cigarette. Even though it had been perfectly innocent, I should have realized how it looked to Lisa. How she felt in that mixed-up, borderline bonkers mind of hers, left standing in the hall, dressed to kill, while I snuck off outside with the object of her affections. OK, so she may have done what she did anyway. The light would presumably still have blown, Gabriel would presumably still have gone up the ladder to fix it – I guess we'll never know. But I do know I have to take at least some of the blame. There's no doubt in my mind that what I did – and what I didn't do, too – pushed her over the edge.

She's left St Mark's, by the way. Not just the Players: the school as well. It turned out her parents were going through a particularly nasty divorce all the while she and I knew each other. She never said a word to me about it, and that's something else I feel bad about. Why didn't she? Isn't that supposed to be what friends are there for, to confide your problems in? (Yeah, OK. I know. What would I know about friendship, and confiding problems? Look at how I didn't confide my problems in Jaz. I *know* all that.)

Anyway, Lisa's mum moved away from Combe Bridge just after Christmas, and Lisa decided to move with her. Fresh start, and all that. So I'll probably never see her again. I'm not sure how I feel about that. Relieved, probably. As well as guilty. Oh, and the word on the street is, she's started seeing somebody about everything that happened – some kind of therapist. Psychiatrist, psychologist, counsellor . . . I'm not sure which. Who *do* you see for having an eating disorder and being a stalker, both at the same time? But she's getting help, at any rate, which I guess is the main thing.

It was Bex's birthday in January, just after the Christmas holidays, and she had a party on the Saturday night, round at the vicarage. For some mad reason, I decided to test out this theory everybody seemed to have, namely that (ahem) Andy fancied me. So I dolled myself up to the nines – as much as I ever doll myself up, that is. I mean I put on a skirt, one of those little flirty flared minis, and spent ages doing my hair and stuff – and went along with a six-pack of Stella and a come-hither smile, and an attitude on me you could smell a mile off.

Well, what can I say? I was right, everybody else was wrong. Andy spent the entire evening playing tonsil tennis with Hollie, and they've been seeing each other ever since. Perhaps it was the unaccustomed sight of my legs that did it. Not that I'm bothered. We always did get on fine and dandy as just mates, and besides, I've kinda gone off boy-girl relationships since all that heavy Lisa/Gabriel stuff. Jaz and Bex were dead disappointed though – the way they carried on about it afterwards, you'd have thought they'd had a bet on. Maybe they did. One thing I do know, it was an amazing party and the three of us had a total blast. It was such a relief to be somewhere Gabriel was and Lisa wasn't. And to have Jaz back again; we spent the whole evening just chilling, and chatting, and dancing. Just like we always used to.

Soon after Bex's party, Mum and Geoffrey called another Family Meeting. Not all officially at the Admiral Benslow, like the last time; this was an informal, round-the-table chat after supper on Friday evening, after Rupert got home for the weekend.

"We've been thinking," Mum began.

"Uh-oh," Moll said. I aimed a kick at her under the table. Not a hard one, just a messing-around one.

"Do go on, Mother Dearest," I said, sweetly. "Just ignore your youngest."

"Geoffrey and I have been taking another look at those estate agents' details." She cast an anxious glance in my direction. "And they really are terribly expensive."

"What, the details?" I pulled a mock-astonished face. "Are they? I always thought estate agents sent them out free of charge."

Moll kicked me back. "Now who's interrupting? Go on, Mother Dearest. We *are* listening, aren't we, Mattie?"

"Course we are. Sorry, Mum."

"That's all right, darling. Do you know, it's so nice to see you in this light-hearted mood. Both of you. It seems ages since I heard you, well, bantering with each other."

"Ooh, yuss," I said, popping a piece of bread into my mouth. "I do like a nice bit o' banter of a Friday evening, don't you, Moll?"

Molly exchanged glances with Rupert, putting a forefinger up to her temple and making screwing movements. "It's quite sad really, isn't it, in one so young?"

"Ha ha." I swallowed the bread. "Meantime," I said to Mum pointedly, "back to the estate agents' details. Is there something you should be telling us?"

"Oh, yes." Mum looked at Geoffrey. "Perhaps you'd better tell them, darling. You know all the ins and outs better than I do."

And Geoffrey told us that they'd decided not to move at all, that all the houses they'd looked at thus far were way too expensive and anyway not really suitable for their needs – for all our needs – and so they'd been looking into having an extension built instead.

"It makes much more sense," he said enthusiastically. "We can extend backwards, into the garden. There's plenty of land there, we won't miss it, and we'll end up with a bigger living space as well as two extra bedrooms, for much less expenditure than moving." He looked at the three of us anxiously. "What do you think?"

"Fab idea!" said Moll. "Does it mean Mat and me can have our own rooms again?"

"Awesome," Rupert said, nodding. "Good plan. As long as it won't be a lot of upheaval. You know, with Alice being pwegnant and everything?"

"Bless you, Rupert." Mum smiled at him. "That's sweet of you to think of that. But don't worry, the building won't start until after the baby's here. I'm sure we'll cope. And yes, Molly, it does mean you and Mattie can have your own rooms again. It will just give us heaps more room altogether. How about you, Mattie?" She looked at me apprehensively. "What do you think?"

It was like everybody was holding their collective breath, waiting for my pronouncement. Heaven knows why. I mean, it's not like I'm the only one whose opinion matters, is it?

"I think it's a brilliant idea," I declared. "Not having to move, a bedroom each plus more living space – what's not to like? Bring it on!"

Afterwards, Geoffrey made Mum go and put her feet up in the sitting room and Molly went off to the kitchen to make some tea, leaving Rupert and me alone together, clearing away the supper things.

"I think that extension idea is bwilliant," he enthused as he collected up the unused cutlery.

"Yeah, me too. I've got really fond of this cottage, you know?" I started stacking the dirty plates. "We've been here for ages. I'd be really sad to leave it."

"It is very pwetty. With the beach being so close, and all."

It was probably the longest conversation the two of us had ever had. And the strange thing was, I didn't feel I particularly wanted to end it.

"I was sorry to hear about Colin," I blurted out, suddenly. "Your rat."

Rupert looked momentarily downcast. "Thanks. He was old and all that, but I do miss him. I was sorry to hear about your fwend, too."

"My friend?" For a moment I didn't know what he meant, thought he'd somehow thought a friend of mine had died, like Colin had. Then I realized. "Oh, you mean Lisa?"

"Mm." He nodded, picking up the water jug and glasses. "Molly told me she's moved away? I guess you're going to miss her."

"In a way, I guess I am. But she wasn't really much of a friend. But then," I added, "I wasn't much of a friend to her, either."

Our eyes met for a long moment. It sounds corny, but it was as if I was looking at him for the very first time. Looking at him properly, I mean.

He gave a rueful grin. "Life just sucks sometimes, doesn't it?"

"It sure does." There was something different about him, something I couldn't put my finger on. "It sucks big banana."

We both started to giggle, even though it wasn't especially funny, and as his giggles turned into laughs, as he threw his head back with a great guffaw, I realized what it was. His braces had gone. He was Tin Grin no more.

Mum poked her head round the door, drawn by the sound of our laughter. By the unusual sound, I suppose.

"Something funny?"

"Not really. Just – just life, I guess." I picked up the plates. "Come on, Rupes. Let's get this job done. Last one to the dishwasher's a sissy."

Don't miss
Catherine Robinson's
fabulous novel

mr perfect

Flora's had it with immature boys. So when she runs into the gorgeous, sophisticated Max it seems like fate. . .

When Hugh got home that afternoon he had a split lip and a livid red-and-purple bruise on his right cheekbone, which he said he'd acquired playing rugby. He seemed unusually reluctant to talk about it though, just grabbed a Fanta and a handful of biscuits and disappeared up to his top-floor eyrie.

But when Nat and Ruby arrived, ten minutes later, they had a rather different explanation. They burst through the front door, the pair of them, agog and fairly frothing with the drama of it all.

"Guess what? Hugh beat Danny up," Nat declared, without preliminaries.

"You're kidding!"

"I'm not, honestly! Am I, Rube?"

"She's not," Ruby confirmed. "Is he home yet?"

"Well, yeah, but –" I thought of what Max had said earlier, about Hugh being useful to have as a brother. I'd thought it was ludicrous, his implication that Hugh might stick up for me with his fists. It had never occurred to me that Max could have been right. "He said he'd been playing rugby," I explained, rather lamely.

"So you've seen his war wounds, then," said Ruby. She sounded satisfied, as if it was her honour that had been avenged, rather than mine.

"Yeah," I said, wonderingly. "God. What did Danny look like?"

"Worse," Ruby pronounced. "Far worse. He had a black eye."

"And he was telling everyone Hugh had broken his nose," Nat added.

"God!" My brother, breaking somebody's nose because of me! I knew I shouldn't approve of violence, but I couldn't help feeling pleased. Just the teensiest bit. Actually, I lie. I was thrilled to bits, over the moon that Danny had got his comeuppance.

"It wasn't broken," Ruby was saying, with scorn, "it was just a bit – you know. Bent."

"So what happened?"

"Hugh just went berserk," Nat breathed, dramatically. "At lunchtime. He came into the common room, went over to where Danny was sitting, and knocked him off his chair. I mean, literally. Like, Pow. Bruce Willis, eat your heart out. Then he piled into him on the floor."

"Really?" I turned to Ruby for confirmation. You could always rely on her to provide a detached viewpoint, a balance to Nat's more sensationalist reporting style.

She nodded. "Pretty much. They were giving it large for about five minutes – nobody dared go near them to break them up. It was full-on warfare – I mean, forget bundles in the playground, this was more like they were re-enacting a scene from Gladiator. Then in came Fozzy and pulled Hugh off Danny, and bawled them both out. Well embarrassing."

"And what happened then?" "Nobody knows," Nat said. "Well, Mr Fosdyke told them both to go and report to him afterwards, but nobody knows what they said to him."

"Or what he said to them," said Ruby. "Nobody saw either of them for the rest of the day. For all we know they've both been suspended. Where is he, anyway?" She craned her neck towards the stairs, as if hoping to catch a glimpse of him. (My brother. My hero. . .)

"Upstairs. In his room. But I'm not going to go and disturb him. I'll ask him about it later on, after you've gone." I knew there was no way Hugh would tell me what had happened while Ruby and Nat were earwigging on the stairs.

"What I don't understand," said Nat, pulling out a stool and sitting on it, "is why Danny wrote that thing in the first place. I mean, the last time we saw you, you and he were like the Romance of the Century; then all of a sudden it's all off, he's bad-mouthing you via the sixth-form noticeboard, and your brother's knocking seven shades of poo out of him. It's like the Montagues and the Capulets all over again."

"No it isn't," I protested. "Romeo and Juliet were in love: Danny and I aren't."

"Well, whaddya know," said Ruby, darkly.

"You are sure it was Danny who wrote it?" Nat said. "Not somebody just wanting to stir up trouble?"

"I'm sure," I said, grimly, and then I told them both exactly what had gone on at Danny's on Sunday. I didn't spare any details, and once again I felt so stupid for not seeing it coming. Stupid and gullible. Predictably, though, Ruby was furious all over again on my behalf.

"He is such a sleazebag! He just assumes you'll be up for a quick shag, and then when you tell him to get lost he says you came on to him, and he never fancied you anyway!"

She has this knack, does Rube, of getting down to the nitty-gritty. Put like that, I could see she had a point; that it was Danny who had the problem, not me.

"That's about it, yeah."

"Forget him," Ruby declared, with a toss of her head. "He might be gorgeous, but he's toxic. You can do better than that. There's loads more guys out there."

"Talking of which," said Nat, "who's this Max who's been answering your phone?"

For a split-second I couldn't think who she meant. It seems incredible, given the galvanizing effect just the mention of his name was to have on me only a short while later; but then, at that time, my head was too full of other thoughts. But when I remembered the events of earlier – me cannoning into him, his kindness to me – I felt an unmistakable but inexplicable blush spread up my neck.

It wasn't wasted on my friends.

"Eh up. Someone interesting, by the look of things," Ruby observed drily.

"Calm down. He's a friend of my parents, they've known him for years."

"That's why she's going red," Nat told her, meaningly.

I ignored her. "He just made sure I was OK, that's all. He's off limits; for a start, he's years older than me."

"That's a big turn-on for some men. You know – the whole Lolita thing."

I hadn't detected anything of the kind from Max. I shook my head. "Nope. Not Max. It wasn't like that – it wasn't, Ruby. Don't look at me in that tone of voice."

"So how old is he, then?" Nat is obsessed with men's ages, she sorts them into categories of suitable or unsuitable depending on their dates of birth, as if that's the only important factor.

"Haven't a clue."

"Well, roughly."

I hazarded a guess. "Twenty-four, twenty-five?"

"It's not that much older."

"Yeah it is. Anyway, forget it. I'm not interested; and even if I was, he certainly isn't. He was just doing the decent thing. He's my parents' friend, for God's sake; it would almost be like incest."

I meant it, too. I really did. I told myself he had simply done what any respectable family friend would have done under the same circumstances – picked me up, dusted me down and set me back on my feet again. Ruby and Nat were creating a liaison where none existed, and there was nothing remotely intriguing about what had happened. Nothing at all.